Collide
By Sarah Hatake

Prologue

It was a dream. Kioshi Hamasaki knew that he was dreaming. Yet it felt so real. He was a spectator of the events going on around him, not a participant. The woman before him did not seem to realize he was even there. Interesting.

There was nothing particularly fetching about the woman. She looked like hell with her dark blonde hair a tangled mess going in every direction. Her eyes were only partially cracked so he was not able to see what color they were. She had just left what he assumed was a bedroom. She must have just woken up... If you could call it that.

He could not help it, he laughed.

She stopped moving and frowned. Did she hear him? She shook her head and went into the bathroom. He started to follow only to have the door shut in his face. He stood outside for a moment, pondering. Where was this place and why was he dreaming of it? It was not any kind of dream he had in the past.

He reached forward and was surprised to see his hand go through the door. He then grinned. He started to walk through then stopped, feeling almost like a pervert looking through the crack in the fence at the bath house.

Kioshi gave a heavy sigh. It was his dream, why shouldn't he spy? Instead of moving forward he wandered down the hallway. The place was decent in size. He saw two more

Sarah Hatake

bedrooms, both empty except for crisply made
beds. They did not appear to have been used in
a while.

Next he found a rather large kitchen.
Some of the items he recognized yet there were
contraptions he had never seen. Funny that his
mind could conjure something so foreign. He
then went into an open area with a large piece of
furniture in it that he assumed was used to sit on.
A large device was opposite of the furniture that
looked like advanced technology. It reminded
him of their broadcasting tech, but he could not
image having something like that in a private
residence.

Another small version was at a corner
desk, a flat device connected to it that had odd
symbols and shapes on it. Foreign language
characters perhaps?

The dream was taking on a bizarre feel to
it. It felt more like he had stepped into another
world rather than a dream.

He frowned and decided to hell with
privacy. The woman had to be the clue to why
he was here. What was his brain trying to tell
him?

Kioshi came to a stop as the bathroom
door abruptly opened in front of him. Eyes that
were a mixture of brown and green greeted him.
Now they were more brown than green, but he
suspected they would become greener depending
upon her mood.

Her hair was now neatly combed and
pulled back into a bun. Her bangs were a bit
longer and would have been in her eyes had she

2

not been wearing glasses. Faint lines about her eyes indicated that she was close to him in age, although to look at her you would assume, she was much younger. She was also tall in comparison to most of the women he had known. He was five foot eleven inches, so he guessed she was maybe four inches shorter than him. Most of the women he had known were much smaller, making him feel like a giant.

She had a cute face, albeit a little plumper than it would have been if she had been her ideal weight. Not that it mattered to him in the least. He was intrigued. Who are you?

He realized that she was frozen in place, staring through him but having a puzzled expression. Almost as if she could sense he was there in front of her...

"Sensei! Kioshi Sensei!"

He jerked awake, a dream after all. He almost fell out of the tree he had been lounging in when he had drifted off to sleep. His book that he had been reading laying open in his lap, his hand still clasping it. He looked down at the student that had yelled up to him, mildly irritated at the interruption.

"What is it Malaki?"

The boy laughed, "You were sleeping weren't you, Sensei?!" He found that extremely amusing and giggled. "If you had been paying attention and not sleeping, you'd see that we've mastered the technique you had shown us."

Kioshi dropped lightly from the tree, shoving the book into his pack on his hip. "Show me."

Chapter One

Raven Karr had the strangest sensation fall over her as she stood in the doorway of her bathroom. It was a strong feeling of being watched. After hearing what sounded like laughter earlier when she woke up, she was a little spooked.

She peered around the corner of the bathroom door to look down the hallway. She strained to hear anything that sounded out of the ordinary. Nothing came to her. She then heard a tick-tick-tick sound coming from her bedroom.

She looked down to see her faithful, if not lazy, red haired dachshund coming towards her. The blanket she had been buried under in the dog bed still stuck to her butt. The dog shook itself, as if trying to wake up, and knocked the blanket to the floor. She then came up excited to her.

Raven laughed, "Good morning to you too."

If anyone had been in the home, Butter would have already been going crazy. Raven frowned and put her hands on her hips. She did not necessarily believe in ghosts, but she was annoyed enough to say, "If someone is here, you get on out of here. I don't want or need your kind of company."

Butter was giving her a look like she was crazy. Raven laughed and started down the hallway. "Need to go outside?"

Her faithful friend began dancing around her feet as she walked to the living room and then the back door. She opened the door and the little dog darted out to take care of her business. Raven closed the door and started packing snacks for work.

She knew she did not need to have so many snacks but really, eating was one of the few pleasures she had in life. Her day in and day out routine was going to work, coming home, watching Anime, maybe working on one of her books, then going to sleep. Repeat. Only on the weekends was it a little different. She would usually clean her place, maybe go for a hike at Purgatory Creek or a stroll along the river, before plopping down in front of the TV or computer to either watch Anime or work on a book.

That was her life. Day in, day out.

Her family lived far away in Iowa. She had been married but her husband had gotten a rare form of cancer and had passed away a few years before. Even when she was married, the routine was almost the same.

Her husband had been a very different person than her. He had been serious, enjoying dramas and true-life stories. He would lay on the couch and watch what he wanted on his phone while she would watch her Anime on the big TV.

Oh, how he had loved her, though. He was not an overly affectionate guy, but she had never doubted that he loved her. They had one child that had died a few years before him, and after that death, he had not been the same. He had lost the will to live. Raven sometimes wondered if that was why he had passed so quickly after being diagnosed with cancer.

For a moment, her eyes burned thinking about her child and husband that had left her alone in the world.

Raven did not know how to not keep fighting. Her entire life had been one uphill battle. She had grown up in a violent home, watching her beautiful mother being beaten so badly that she was unrecognizable, for most of her adolescence. She had shied away from men because of the fear of marrying someone like her ex-stepfather. That fear coupled with her lack of confidence due to her continual fight with her weight, she was thirty before she had started dating.

Her mother had finally left the relationship, but Raven was an adult by then. They had moved North to Iowa, and it was there where her mother met the man that Raven would regard as her father. Had it not been for him, she would never had taken a chance on men.

She had met Riley by chance, and they got married within a year. Their daughter, Leia, was born a few years later. She had suddenly become sick and within a few hours had died. Later they would learn that the fluid that cushioned the brain had backed up causing pressure to her brain. It literally crushed her brain. The doctors could not pinpoint why she had become so sick so quickly and had assumed it was the flu. They had sent them home. She died in Raven's arms as she was waiting for the ambulance to arrive. Riley had been at work.

Even after that trauma, Raven had not known how to give up. If anything, Leia's death had made her want to dig in deeper. The trauma was more than any one person should experience. She still had nightmares of those last moments and flashbacks when something triggered the memory. No one should bury their own child, especially one so little. She could understand on one level why Riley had given up, but it was so contrary to the strong will she had been born with that she had a hard time accepting it.

"Damn it, Riley, why couldn't you fight for me?" she whispered to the empty room, not for the first time.

It had caused a great pain in her soul that her husband, although he loved her, could not overcome his depression even for her. She gave a heavy sigh. The cancer had been a blessing for him, he had wanted to go on the moment their baby girl had died. Nothing was going to change that.

Raven went to the back door and let Butter back in. She danced around, wanting her carrot treat for taking care of business. The little dog made her laugh and kept the loneliness at bay. She had been a gift after Riley's passing from her best friend, Mark, and his wife, Amber.

She tossed a carrot piece to her, went back into the living room and turned on the tv. She left it on the all-day Anime channel to comfort Butter while she was gone to work.

"You be good, Butter," she said as she grabbed her bag and went out the door.

Raven leaned back in her chair, watching the video conversations going on between inmates and their friends or family. Outside her enclosed room, in-person visits were going on as well; however, it was the correctional officers keeping an eye on those visits. Between checking in new visitors, monitoring the online visits, and reviewing new applicants, she was able to work on her novels with the inevitable lull.

She really enjoyed working at the Jail overall. Her position kept her relatively isolated. She interacted with those that were checking in but being located where she was, the other employees had a tendency of forgetting she existed. That was fine by her. She enjoyed working by herself without the unnecessary drama that always went with side by side work.

As she was getting older, she noticed that she enjoyed simplicity. Not to say that she did not like being with others. She always had a great time with her best friend and his wife. She also enjoyed talking with her family. They had not been happy when she had chosen to stay in Texas after Riley's death. Yet, she knew she was better on her own. She was able to do whatever she wanted, whenever she wanted without explanation.

It was lonely but she had learned something in her life. People eventually would leave you. Clinging too tightly would not keep them at your side. It was better to be alone and at peace rather than with someone and in turmoil.

The last years before his death after their
daughter's passing, had been painful. It was hard
living with someone who was in a continual place
of darkness. Especially for someone like her,
who as an empath, would feel the emotions as
her own. She had tried everything to get him
focused on something to live for, but nothing had
worked. His only outlet was his phone and social
media. They made love infrequently because
even that desire had left. They were almost more
like roommates for a time.

Just before he had gotten sick, there was
a turning point in which they had what had felt
like a second honeymoon. He was more
loveable and was not under quite as dark a cloud.
Yet she was always aware that he had no will to
live. Her ability as an empath could discern, he
was just going through the motions. Then he got
sick and when they got the diagnosis, while he
tried to hide it, she could see and feel that he was
happy that his end was near. He refused
treatment and within six months he was gone.

Raven pushed the memories aside. It
did not matter anymore. It was done and over
with. This was her life now. Her mind drifted as
the song playing on Pandora caught her attention.
She briefly closed her eyes, unconsciously
moving in tune with the song in her seat. She
loved music. She had been stuck on a spot in her
novel and as she listened to the music images
suddenly began flashing through her mind.

She grinned and sat up, instantly opening
the novel she was working on and started typing
furiously. She laughed at the scene that had

come to her. This book was different than the ones she had written before and her protagonist male was about to get himself into some serious trouble with the heroine.

Butter was excited as she came through the door that night. She took her out and stood in the back yard as a strong wind blew around them. It was a nice night. She was half tempted to stay out back for a longer period but dismissed it. As lovely as it was, she was ready to get out of her clothes and into her pajamas. It was her routine.

Butter ran back having completed her business and Raven turned to walk back inside. The strange sensation of being watched fell over her again but she shrugged it off. If some ghost had nothing better to do than stalk her so be it. So long as it left her alone, she would share her space.

Maybe that was what her next novel should be about. She mused over it as she walked to the back and hastily pulled her uniform off. She scowled at her semi-naked image in the mirror. "Gag, I wouldn't want to be with me." She grabbed the bit of fat on her belly and moved it up and down. "Good thing I'm not looking for anyone. This would be embarrassing."

Kioshi snorted, barely able to restrain his laughter. What a weird set of dreams he was having. She was an unusual woman, that much was sure. While she was speaking another language, for whatever reason he could understand her. Perhaps because it was his dream.

He instinctively stepped back as she left the bathroom to go into her bedroom. He was not at all ashamed at looking at her almost naked form. He appreciated women of all shapes and sizes. He followed her and watched as she pulled on what looked like sleepwear. He looked at the light in the window and raised a brow. It was rather early to be going to sleep. He looked around the room in curiosity as she muttered to herself.

The bed was rather large for just her. He grinned as he noticed a long pillow in the middle of the un-made bed. It was clear that she snuggled the pillow at night. She had some figurines on one bookcase, he assumed they had some significance to her. Another one of those technological devices as she had in the other room sat on top of the bookcase.

Along one wall was an image of a turbulent ocean with lightning streaking across the sky. He had to admit it was one of the most real pictures he had ever seen. He wondered how the artist had captured such a realistic scene. He shifted his gaze to the wall behind her bedframe and froze.

A large colorful drawing of a man in a fighting pose hung in the center of the wall above the bed. That man was him! Beneath the image was his own name in large, bold letters.

"What the hell?!" he thundered.

Raven froze as she once again she thought she heard a voice. She looked around the room. She was very much alone except for Butter who had flopped onto her doggie bed as she was straightening up the room. The lack of the dog's response made her question her own sanity.

"I must be losing it," she muttered. She looked at the image of her favorite anime character hanging over the bed. She smiled as she looked at it. "God... If you were only real Kioshi." She giggled and covered her mouth. "I'm seriously crazy. Who am I kidding anyway? Even if he was real, he'd never give me two looks." She chuckled while shaking her head, "And I would lack the confidence to even approach him. I might make friends with him, but I'd pine away like always in secret."

Raven covered her face with a moan, "I'm hopeless."

Her phone buzzed on the bed. She picked it up and read the message on the screen. She grinned, another special Funko Pop release that Mark was keeping her in the loop about. She typed back a quick response and started to put the phone back, but he messaged again.

What are you doing this weekend?

Same as always. Lol.

Come over, you haven't been by in a while. We're grilling some huge steaks.

Raven made a face. That would require getting out of her pajamas for the weekend. She then grinned, she always enjoyed hanging out with them.

Alright, I'll come. What time you want me to come?

We'll be up by 10 so any time after that.

She gave a big thumbs up then closed the app. She turned to leave the room and felt energy roll over her. A strong sense of frustration and irritation hit her in a wave.

"That's weird," she muttered. "I definitely must be losing it. Come on, Butter, let's go watch some TV."

Kioshi was beyond frustrated now. He had thought for a moment that she had seen him when she addressed him. Then he realized she was talking to the drawing over the bed. Then he got irritated. I'm right here! He muttered but she obviously did not hear him this time. And who the hell are you and where did you get that picture of me?

He was not able to step back as she abruptly turned around after moving her fingers over a small device in her hands. She walked right through him and he was hit with the sense of her spirit in that moment. Loneliness. She hesitated for a moment and he realized with her words after that she had indeed felt his presence. She was dismissing it, however, thinking she was imagining it.

He followed her down the hallway and into the main room. She sat down on the large piece of furniture and turned on the piece of technology. He was surprised to see images on the screen that appeared for entertainment purposes. He hesitated for a moment before

13

climbing over the back of the piece of furniture and sitting down next to her.

Kioshi was apparently stuck where he was at for the time being. He might as well relax until he either woke up or the dream shifted into something else. He shoved his hands into his pockets and propped his legs up on the same leg rest she was stretched out on.

She used a small, rectangular object to control the device. She pulled up a drawing show of some sort and started. He almost came off the seat when he saw drawings of people that he knew personally. These were images of events that had happened in the past. He then was shocked as he saw his own likeness, talking just as he talked but in animation.

He turned to look at her and was stunned at the way she was looking at him on the screen. She gave a long sigh and bit her lower lip before saying, "Damn, you're so awesome. I really wish you were real. Even if I'd be a coward, at least I could see you and get to know you for real."

Kioshi jerked as he suddenly came awake. He was sweating and the moonlight was drifting into the room while a breeze caressed his warm skin. The sweet smell of jasmine that grew outside his window wafted over him. He had been dreaming but it was not just a dream. He was certain of it. That place, that woman, they were real.

He lifted his hand to his forehead and smoothed his hair back as he tried to make sense of what he had seen. What did that even mean?

In that place, they were just animations for the people's entertainment?

He was confused and disturbed all at the same time. The images were from the past, when he was in his late twenties. The scene had been exactly as it had happened. Seeing himself in a drawing form interacting on the device she called a TV was highly disturbing to him as well. How much of his life had been the product of entertainment?

Going off her expression, he was thinking quite a bit. She was obviously infatuated with him... or rather, the drawing that she was watching... which was still him. He laughed at the absurdity of the thought but knowing it was an accurate assessment.

It was rather flattering when he thought about it. She could not have been infatuated with his body because it was a drawing and only had some of his characteristics not all. It had to be who he was as an individual and that gave him some pause.

Who are you?

Kioshi sat up in bed, grabbed his pants that were folded neatly on the nightstand before getting into them. He then pulled on a sleeveless undershirt and walked towards the door. He had to talk to someone about what he had seen. Only one person could he think of to talk to, the current leader of their village, his former student, and the savior of the world, Naozumi.

Chapter Two

Naozumi Tanaka was still in his office, even though it was in the middle of the night. There was so much paperwork and requests for assistance, the he just could not keep up with it. If he had realized that there was so much paperwork in running a village, he might have found a new goal to shoot for as a kid.

He rubbed his eyes and yawned. His wife was going to kill him for being gone another night, especially since they were expecting their first child. He wanted to get ahead of the paperwork, though, before their child was born so that he could be home helping her.

He sensed his Sensei before he saw him. "Kioshi, what brings you by this time of night?"

"I should ask you why you're here this late. I thought I was going to have to wake you at home."

"There is just so much paperwork... I'm about to go crazy if you must know," he said while grinning at the older man. "How did you keep up with it all?"

Kioshi's dark eyes crinkled at the corners from amusement and Naozumi knew he was smiling beneath his face mask. He tilted his head to the side, "Honestly, I dumped half of it on my assistant and anything that was not an emergency I delegated to others to take care of."

Naozumi laughed, "I should do the same, old man, before Hikari gives me her fists of thunder."

Something serious was bothering his former Sensei. While he smiled at the words, his stance and expression were very serious. The old man, as he called him, was not really that old. He was in his early forties to Naozumi's twenty, which is why he called him an old man.

His Sensei's hair was silver in color and always in a perpetual state of spiky disarray. Even though his hair was that color, it had nothing to do with his age. He had always had that color of hair, even as a child. It was a family trait that all the men in his family shared.

He was still in very good shape, even after having spent a few years in the same position that Naozumi now held. His Sensei was a dangerous and powerful man when he was called into action. If it had not been for Kioshi, he might not have become the savior of the world as he had or accomplished any of the goals he had chased after so diligently.

"What is bothering you, Sensei?" he finally asked.

The older man raked his gloved hand through his hair in a show of frustration before dropping down in the chair across from him. "I've been having these dreams."

Naozumi raised his brows, "Dreams?"

"It's a dream but... not like anything I have ever had before. It's not just a dream, Naozumi, it's real."

He leaned back in his chair and listened as Kioshi described everything he had seen and experienced. He did not know what to say at first, so he remained silent as he carefully thought over everything.

"I wonder..." he finally said while leaning forward. "I wonder Sensei where our stories come from. Where the thoughts and ideas are formed. You read a lot, where do you think the ideas come from."

Kioshi gave a slight grin, "The stories I read are born from a perverted mind."

Naozumi laughed hard, "Bad example."

"Very bad example."

"We know that there are other dimensions after our fight with Masa that almost destroyed our world," Naozumi said after a momentary pause. "What if every story ever written, in whatever dimension it is written in, is actually born from a real place."

Kioshi frowned at the idea, "I do not find it pleasing that everything we have suffered, fought for, and for some of our comrades died for, is entertainment for others. It angers me thinking that somewhere people are finding enjoyment from our suffering."

Naozumi's blue eyes seemed to almost glow when he met his Sensei's eyes, "They could also find hope through us, though, Kioshi Sensei. Is that not an amazing thought?"

Kioshi had to smile at the words. Leave it to Naozumi to find the gold lining. He had never known a person as positive as him, even in the darkest of moments. The kid had grown up into an impressive man. He felt pride that he had been a part of his growing years.

"I suppose that is true," he conceded. "The woman I saw she was very... engrossed in our story. I had the impression that she lives a rather solitary life."

"Like someone else I know," Naozumi remarked.

Kioshi chuckled, "That will not be changed." He sighed before coming back to the main point of his visit, "Why am I seeing this, Naozumi? I'm not given to visions or things of this nature."

Naozumi folded his hands together. "I wonder if our two worlds are very close together right now. Perhaps because she is so focused on our world that is why you are seeing her world."

Kioshi felt his cheeks warm. It appeared she was exceptionally focused on *him*. If Naozumi was correct, it would make sense that he personally would be shown what he was shown.

"I wouldn't worry about it," Naozumi concluded. "If that is the case, eventually the two worlds with drift apart again and you will stop having these dreams."

"What if I get stuck in her world somehow?"

Naozumi chuckled, "That could get interesting. I would suggest when you go to sleep that you put yourself into a state where you can immediately awaken if that seems to be a possibility."

Kioshi gave a heavy sigh, "Thank you for that suggestion. I had not thought of it. I will do as you say."

"So.... What did I look like?"
Kioshi laughed at the question.

Raven woke with a start. She turned her
eyes to the tv and saw that it was already nine in
the morning. She stared at the ceiling for a long
moment. That was a strange dream. She might
be watching too much of her favorite anime,
Naozumi. She normally did not have dreams of
being in that place and especially not dreams
where she was an observer not a participant.
When she had dreams, she was entertaining her
2D crush.

What they were talking about was exactly
what she had been writing about in her most
recent series of books. She had obviously been
thinking too much about it lately and it was
starting to bleed over into her favorite anime.

Raven flung the blanket off herself and
pushed herself up. She groaned, her neck a little
sore from sleeping in an awkward position.
Butter jumped up immediately when she saw her
legs swing over the side of the bed. She quickly
pulled on a pair of pajama bottoms, slipped her
slides on, and walked out of the bedroom to the
back door.

Butter shot out fast, having needed to go
bad. She was such a good dog, never making
messes in the house. Raven yawned and slowly
made her way into the kitchen, turning on her
coffee machine after dropping a pod in the slot,
and went to the refrigerator.

"Ugh..." Nothing looked appealing. She
would grab a taco on the road. She grabbed a

chopped carrot and shut the door before walking back to let Butter in. "That's a good girl. We're going to see Mark and Amber today. Won't that be fun?"

Butter wagged her tail and looked up at her with adoring eyes. Raven laughed, "I sure do love you, you little ray of sunshine."

"Did you hear what our government has been working on that got leaked?" Mark asked her as he poked one of the large steaks on the grill.

"Here we go," Amber said with a laugh. "I'm going to get another drink."

Raven laughed at her hasty exist. She had obviously heard this one too many times. She smiled as she watched her abruptly change course to chase after their son, Rider, who was in turn chasing Butter around the yard.

"No, I have not been paying attention to the news," Raven said with a grin. "I've been working on a few novels and if I do watch TV it's Naozumi."

"I created a monster," Mark said with a laugh.

Raven had to agree. If it was not for Mark, she never would have gotten into anime let alone watched Naozumi the first time. She had several anime's that she loved but by far it was her favorite and mostly due to her obsession with Kioshi.

"What have they been up to?"

"Apparently, they have discovered a way of tapping into other dimensions," he responded.

Raven groaned and covered her face with her hand, "Are you serious? This is NOT the year for that. We've had global pandemics, averted a few wars, riots, political unrest, and now they're going to be messing with other dimensions?"

Mark laughed, "I thought you'd be excited by that. You might get a chance to jump into Naozumi."

She rolled her eyes, "Please. Just because I write stories that theorize that other dimensions are where our stories come from, doesn't mean I believe it. Our luck, we'll get invaded by warfarin aliens."

He laughed and started scooping the steaks off the grill onto plates. "You are probably right about that." He grinned at her, "If you do disappear, I'm not looking for you."

Raven laughed, "Fair enough."

Several hours later, Raven came home with a full belly and about a drink short of a buzz. She loved spending time with her friends when they were all able to get together. They were such a cute couple and complemented one another so well. Their son was a joy to watch and play with too. When she played with him, her ache over losing Leia lessened.

She leaned back against her door and turned the lock. She had cut herself off at their home because she had to drive home. Now that she was home though...

She grinned and almost ran into her kitchen. She pulled out a Naozumi glass from the cabinet, then reached up and pulled out a

bottle of Salted Caramel Crown Royal. She filled
the glass half-way up with the sweet whiskey
before putting the liquor back in the cabinet. She
then pulled a cold bottle of coke out of the fridge
and filled it the rest of the way up. She dropped a
straw into the glass last.

Raven hurried back to the living room,
kicked off her shoes, and sat down on the couch.
She flipped the TV on and started her show back
up. She was in the middle of re-watching it from
the beginning. She was still in their teen years,
when Kioshi was their Sensei.

The straw might not have been the best
idea because she drank it a lot faster than she
would have if she had been drinking it straight
from the glass. It did not take long before her
body was humming, and she was very relaxed.

Raven gave a long sigh as she looked at
Kioshi on the screen. She absolutely adored and
loved him. After all the hell he had gone through
in life and yet he never complained. He lived a
solitary life which she did not think was fair. He
deserved someone who would love him and give
him children. He would be an amazing father.

"Damn, Kioshi, why you never give a girl
a chance? You should be a father. You
practically raised Naozumi and look at how
awesome he turned out. You deserve
happiness."

*Kioshi was touched by her words more
than he ever would have admitted to another
person. She set her almost empty glass down and
leaned her head on her arm. A sad smile was on*

*her face as she watched the show. She was
starting to nod off, the little red dog had curled
up against her.*

*"I haven't found one worth going after,"
he answered her, not expecting her hear him.*

*Her eyes were closed but her lips
twitched, "So you say. I believe you don't think
you're good enough to have love. That the things
you've done excludes you from happiness."*

He straightened; she had heard him!

*She gave a little giggle, "I must be really
drunk because I swear, I heard him say that."
She rolled onto her side, facing the back of the
furniture. The little dog shifted and curled into
the small space between her and the cushions.*

*"You did hear me," he responded,
leaning closer to her. "What is your name?"*

*She grinned a little, her voice sleepy.
"Raven. My name is Raven."*

*"Raven," he reached to shake her. If she
could hear him then he had questions. He
frowned in frustration as his hand went right
through her. "Raven don't go to sleep just yet. I
need to ask you some questions."*

*He sighed when he realized it was too
late. She was already passed out. He folded his
hands together and closed his eyes before saying,
"Release!"*

Kioshi opened his eyes, seeing that light
was beginning to slowly fill his bedroom. It was
still very early in the morning. He smiled slightly,
at least now he knew her name.

"Raven," he spoked softly.

He had never heard the name before, it was unique like she was. She had seen exactly how he felt. He did not deserve happiness or love. He had made many mistakes in his life. By his own hand, he had killed an innocent angel who was also his friend. His best friend had died protecting him. He had failed so many times at great cost to those he loved and cared for. No, he did not deserve happiness. Nor could he ever allow himself to love because that person would be in danger. Death followed him and he was the harbinger of death.

No, he could never love or be a father. He would not know the first thing about being a father. His own father had killed himself when he was four years old. He had been the one to find him and it had shattered him inside. From that moment forward, he had raised himself and forged his own path.

It was a solitary path and must remain so.

Kioshi sat up in his bed. Across the room he saw his reflection in the mirror. He stared at himself for a long while, his body was a testimony to the life of violence and death. His torso was covered in scars. He would have more on his legs. He looked down at his hands. His fingers were long and slender. While they did not look strong, they were in fact instruments of death.

His chakra coiled and collected in his hand at the thought. His hand became encased in electrical energy. He closed it into a fist and the chakra dissipated immediately. Raven had rattled his thoughts.

He rolled out of the bed and pulled on his clothes. As soon as he had everything on, he ran out the door. He ran along the path he did every morning; the cool air was brisk that early. He was running as much from his thoughts as he was from Raven's words.

Raven groaned, her head pounding. Her body made a few cracking sounds as she straightened up on the couch. She winced, "Getting old sucks."

She sputtered as Butter started licking her all over her face. She squinted as she pushed the little dog back. Butter obviously had enjoyed sleeping with her on the couch. She rolled off the couch and walked towards the back door, half asleep still. She opened the door for Butter then started moving slowly down the hallway to the bathroom.

"What is your name?"

She stopped halfway down the hallway as the memory of Kioshi's voice came back to her. She rubbed her eyes and shook her head. "I really am a Simp..." She chuckled as she continued to the bathroom, "A really drunk Simp."

After a long shower and getting herself pulled together, she remarkably felt pretty good. She leaned close to the mirror, looking unhappily at the faint lines that were beginning to form around her eyes. Her youth was slipping away. It did not seem that long ago that she was a teenager.

She gave a heavy sigh before running the brush through her shoulder length hair then pulling it up into a ponytail. She pulled her longer bangs out, helping to make herself look a little bit younger than her forty-three years.

Raven refused to wear makeup. She was allergic to most makeup and the makeup she could wear always seemed to make her look older rather than younger. Riley had also disliked makeup, so she never wore it. She was too old to change that now.

After treating her body so badly the night before, she knew that she needed to go for a walk. It would do Butter some good to get out of the house too. She was starting to get a little fat from being inside all the time.

She checked the temperature on her phone and grabbed a hoodie. She was dressed in her favorite Kioshi t-shirt, jeans that were half a size too big because she had been losing weight, tennis shoes, and now her Wind Village themed hoodie. She grabbed her headphones, shoving them into her hoodie pocket next to her cellphone.

Butter was excited when she put on her harness and leash. She got in the car without any trouble and only mildly made Raven crazy with her excited whining on the way to Purgatory Creek. There were only a few vehicles in the early morning hours.

Raven looked around the parking lot as she got out. She tugged her pants leg up and secured first her ankle holster, then slid her .380 into the holster. She had worked long enough at the jail to know it was foolish for a woman to go out and about without some form of protection. She tugged her pants leg back down over the weapon that was locked and loaded. She then pulled her headphones out, sliding them into her ears before connecting them to her cellphone. She started her exercise playlist, which consisted of high energy music from bands such as Imagine Dragons, Fall Out Boy, and the like. She opened the back door to release Butter.

The little girl dove out of the backseat in her zeal and Raven almost missed grabbing her leash. She laughed, "Boy, you sure are wound up today." She shut the door and depressed the lock on her fob.

It was a little chilly that morning, but it did wonders to wake Raven up as she started down the walking trail. As she came to the three forked trails, she turned down her favorite. It was a denser trail and made her feel like she was going back in time. The music was really getting her pumped as she went further and further down the trail. Her mind wandered.

She was switching Butter's leash to her other hand when the little dog suddenly yanked free of her grip, chasing a squirrel through the brush off the path.

"Butter!" she yelled before giving pursuit.

The little dog did not give heed to her yell and kept chasing the animal. Raven cursed as she tried to keep up with Butter, an impossible task because the little dog was like lightning. She rounded a tree just as she noticed a strange light in the distance.

It looked almost like the air itself was splitting open and immediately she was reminded of the conversation she had with Mark the day before. She watched in horror as Butter and the squirrel were running right towards it.

"No! Butter!" she screamed and doubled her speed to catch up to the little dog.

Raven watched in horror as the squirrel then Butter disappeared into the now large rip in time and space. She shook, unsure what she should do. Dimly she could see the outline of trees, but they seemed a very far distance away.

"Oh god, oh god, oh god...What do I do?" she whispered. "Butter!"

Tears were freely falling down her cheeks and her limbs shook in fear as she looked at the opening directly before her. She looked to the heavens before making a rather rash decision as she noticed the opening was beginning to close.

"God help me," she whispered before diving through the opening just before it shut.

She felt as if her body had converted into pure energy as she spun and twisted in a colander of blue light. She could not even fathom how fast she must have been traveling. It was quite beautiful and for a moment, she wondered if she would be locked inside it forever.

Abruptly a brilliant flash of light blinded her eyes and she felt her body reforming into herself and sailing through the air. She hit solid dirt hard, knocking the wind out of her lungs, and then kept rolling from the momentum.

Her body finally came to a sliding stop and she did not move. The music she had been listening to was suddenly very loud and she shakily reached up and pulled the headphones out. A canopy of trees was overhead, and she could only stare at them and wonder where the portal had taken her.

Butter's face appeared in front of her before she started licking her. Raven groaned and pushed her back. She was thankful they had survived whatever that portal had been.

Kioshi came to an abrupt halt as he saw the air splitting open into what looked like a portal. He had seen those before in the last great war. He hopped onto the nearest tree and crouched, wondering if anything would come through. He kept his hand near his pouch where his kunai and other weapons were located.

He blinked as a furry, brown squirrel came out first. It looked around before running up a nearby tree. Not even a second later out came a little red dog that looked very much like the one that Raven had came flying out.

"Interesting."

The little red dog began sniffing the ground, obviously still wanting to chase the first animal to come through. He started to lower his hand as the portal began to close when suddenly in a burst of light a person emerged.

They hit the ground hard, rolling a few times before sliding to a stop. They lay still for a long moment and the little red dog suddenly noticed their arrival and started running towards them. They reached up and pulled something out of their ears but did not sit up or move. The little red dog was licking their face and after a moment they pushed the dog away with a groan. They finally sat up and shook their head. They reached up and pulled the hood of their outer garment down. Kioshi almost fell out of the tree when he saw her face.

Chapter Three

Raven looked around at the densely wooded area. The trees were very different than the ones on her trail in Texas. These were very tall and old looking. Her arm was sore as she rubbed it. It had taken the brunt of her entry into the new location. Her vision was a little fuzzy because her glasses had obviously come off when she came through.

She pulled her phone out of her pocket and shut off the music. She then looked at the signal and felt a small measure of fear. Not only was there no signal, it did not even say she was roaming. She had been overseas with Riley to visit his family in Ireland just before Leia had died. Her phone had not worked there either, but it had said roaming.

"Oh shit," she whispered. "Butter, what have you gotten me into now?"

The little dog danced around and was so cute that she could not stay mad at her for long. She absently rubbed her aching arm before she carefully got to her feet and started looking for her glasses.

"This would be so much easier if I could see," she muttered, not lost on the irony of the statement.

"Are these what you are looking for?"

Raven's heart almost stopped at the very familiar voice that came out of nowhere. She spun around and jumped back at the same time.

She gave a small shriek as she lost her footing and fell back on her ass once more.

He knelt in front of her, meeting her eye level. She was in wordless shock as she looked at the man that was so close to her. It was impossible but... he looked exactly like Kioshi. At least, how she had always imagined Kioshi would look like if he was more than a two-dimensional person.

The spiky silver hair that was kept back by an elaborate headband was a little moist, as if he had been exercising recently. It was in sharp contrast to his slightly darker toned skin that had a golden undertone. His eyes were almond shaped with thick lashes and eyes that were so dark they seemed almost black except she could now see that they were in fact a shade of gray.

At the corner of his eyes, faint smile lines were noticeable indicating his age. They crinkled as they looked at her and she had the impression that he was smiling, even though she could not see the lower half of his face because of the mask he was wearing.

"Hello, Raven, nice to meet you in person finally," he then said while offering her glasses to her. His voice was identical to the show, even the inflections. "This must all be a shock to you right now."

Shock was an understatement. She could not even speak as she looked at the man she had adored as an anime. She wordlessly took the glasses and put them on. His image came into better focus and she was speechless.

Kioshi gave a soft chuckle, "I promise I won't bite." He tilted his head to the side, "Unless you want me to."

Raven gasped, "What?"

He laughed, "You found your tongue. That is excellent. I must admit, I was rather surprised to see it was you that had come out of the portal. I am glad, though. I have been wanting to ask you questions, Raven."

She shook her head, "Wait, wait, wait. You're Kioshi Hamasaki, correct?"

"In the flesh," he grinned.

"And you know my name.... how?" she asked with even more confusion.

"You told me, just last night," he chuckled. "Do you not remember talking with me before you fell asleep?"

Raven felt her face turn warm as a blush spread across her face. "You were really there? That was really your voice?"

His dark eyes smiled into her own, "Yes. Our two dimensions have been very close to one another. I have visited you a few times, unintentionally, in my dreams because of this. Last night was one of those times, except this time you heard me talking to you. Perhaps it was the alcohol you consumed that enabled you to finally hear me?"

Raven was mortified as she wondered at what times he had been present with her. His eyes crinkled as he guessed the nature of her thoughts. Those eyes shifted from hers down the length of her body and he chuckled as he looked at his own image on her shirt.

"As I said, I have many questions for you."

He straightened and extended his hand to her. She hesitantly took his hand and he easily pulled her to her feet. She smiled in thanks before brushing her pants off.

"Turn around," he said softly.

She hesitated before doing as he asked. He gently brushed off the back of her hoodie. He certainly felt real. His hands paused on her shoulders and she turned to look at him. He was looking at the large emblem on the back of her hoodie.

"You truly are a unique woman," he finally said. "I should take you to the village. Our leader will want to meet you."

Kioshi led the way as they walked towards the village. He was half tempted to take her to his place instead. The thought had surprised him earlier as he had dusted off the leaves and dirt that had gotten on her back from her tumble. He had been surprised when he felt a twinge of arousal from just barely touching her.

He had forced the thoughts that had risen to his mind away, back into that forbidden place he kept tightly under control. She thankfully had misinterpreted what he was thinking. He stayed ahead of her so he would not be tempted again.

"Kioshi, thank you for helping me. If you hadn't been around, I don't know what I might have done."

He looked over his shoulder at her. She at some point had scooped up the little dog and had her tucked in her arms. "Why did you enter the portal?"

She blinked, "Butter."

"Excuse me?"

She laughed, "My dog's name is Butter. We were on a hike and she got loose from me and was chasing a squirrel. I watched them run into that... portal... and I didn't know what to do honestly. It started closing and I just couldn't lose her. I saw trees through the opening and hoped for the best."

"That was reckless thing to do for an animal," he responded.

"She's all I have," Raven said softly. "I've lost everything else. I just couldn't lose her too."

He stopped, hearing the pain in the words. It was a pain that he could understand all too well. "I'm sorry."

She cleared her throat, "It's okay. I have her still and now I've got to meet you too."

Kioshi looked over his shoulder and smiled, "You might not feel that way when you cannot return to your own world."

Raven grinned her mood noticeably lightened, "Never. You have no idea how excited I am to be here. I love this world."

"We shall see," he responded. "There is more to our world that just what you have seen on your... TV."

"Hey..." she had grabbed his hand, stopping him.

36

Raven could feel a tiny bit of anger coming from him in his words. She reacted without thinking, taking hold of his hand. It was warm and callused. She blinked as he turned back towards her in response. She almost plowed into him.

She lost her thought being so close to him. She had to mentally shake herself as his dark eyes bore into her.

"I honestly mean what I said with full respect," she finally said. "I have nothing but love for your village and people. In my darkest time, it gave me something to cling onto. Naozumi's example made me see that there was always hope if we just didn't give up. It was never just a show for me. I came to love y'all very much."

Kioshi watched as a blush crossed her features.

"I'm sorry for all that you have suffered, Kioshi. If any good came from it, it was that I learned to never complain even when things were awful. You taught me that. You never complained. You never wailed about how unfair it was. You just kept going, fighting for what was right. Never deviating from the right path even though you had every reason to do so. You have no idea how much I needed that when my daughter died and then later my husband."

He was stunned by her words. He was even more shocked to learn that she had lost greatly as well. "I'm sorry."

Raven cleared her throat and looked away from him when she thought she might cry.

"It has been a few years now. I just wanted you to understand that you weren't just entertainment for me. I needed your story to get through my own."

Kioshi stunned her, and himself in the process, as he suddenly wrapped her in his arms and held her tight. He smelled like mint and freshly chopped wood. Raven closed her eyes, enjoying the feel of his strong arms around her. If this was a dream, she hoped she never work up from it. She never wanted it to end.

Kioshi was not sure why he had suddenly held her. It was not at all like himself. As she leaned into him, he could smell the lingering aroma of something sweet. Her arms wrapped around him and squeezed tight.

He was stunned when he realized she was crying. Her next words floored him because it was not her situation she was crying about, but rather for him.

"You went through so much hell alone. You didn't deserve that, Kioshi. I'm so sorry that happened to you. You have no idea how many times I wanted to comfort you. And now you are trying to comfort me." Raven abruptly pulled away from him and hastily wiped at her eyes. "I'm sorry if I embarrassed you. I know you're a very private man."

She stepped around him and continued in the direction they had been heading leaving him speechless in her wake.

As they entered the village, Raven began to feel conspicuous in her clothes and hastily zipped the front of her hoodie up, hiding the shirt with his image emblazoned on it. Kioshi made a coughing sound at the action but did not say anything. His eyes were crinkled though, and she had the distinct feeling he was laughing.

She hoped to god he did not know that she had a major crush on him. That he only thought it was admiration and nothing more. Knowing him as she did, she knew that he did not want a relationship with anyone. It would just be a major rejection and embarrassment if he knew how much she lusted after him. She had to admit to herself that it was even more so since she was with him in person. He was breathtaking to her.

Raven was in awe as they walked through the streets. She saw so many faces that she recognized. It was strange seeing them as real people and not animations. When she caught sight of the iconic ramen restaurant, her mouth watered. When she got some money together, that would be her first stop.

Since she was with Kioshi, no one really questioned who she was, they just accepted her. She recognized the tall tower of the village headquarters and her heart skipped a beat. She was going to meet Naozumi! She could barely contain her excitement the closer they got.

Kioshi glanced over at her, "Are you nervous?"

"No, I'm so excited," she eagerly answered. "I can't believe I'm going to meet Naozumi!"

Kioshi's silver brows shot up at her excitement, "This should prove to be interesting."

Naozumi looked up as Kioshi casually entered his office, his hands tucked into his pockets. He was much more at ease than he had been the other night, which was a relief. What he did not expect is the woman that came in behind him.

Her eyes were wide as she looked back at him. She was biting her lower lip, clutching her hands together, and looked ready to pop with... excitement? She was a stark contrast to Kioshi who looked bored.

"Kioshi?" he questioned.

"Remember the woman I was talking about the other night?" He pulled one hand out of his pocket to point a thumb at her. "This is her. Raven... this is Naozumi."

"Oh. My. God." She said with a growing smile. "It's really you. I can't believe it's really you."

He stood and came around his desk. "It's nice to meet you, Raven."

Raven took his offered hand eagerly and laughed. "You are so freaking awesome."

Naozumi felt his cheeks warm as she shook his hand enthusiastically. He raised his other hand to his head and laughed, "Ah, well, thank you." He looked at Kioshi who appeared to have checked out of the conversation. He had his book pulled out and was looking at it rather than them. "How did you come here?"

Raven smiled and picked up a little red dog from the ground. "This is Butter. She was chasing a squirrel and went through some kind of portal. I went after her and here I am. I know I should be scared to be here but I'm so excited. I've loved the wind village and all of y'all for so long, I feel like I've come home."

Naozumi grinned, "It's a great village, believe it!"

Kioshi stared at his book as the two of them had a rather energetic talk. He did not think he would ever meet anyone that could match Naozumi's energy, but he was wrong. He would fire a question her way, she would answer, and then fire one off herself. They went back and forth with one another a good twenty minutes before their mutual excitement died down to an appropriate level.

He was startled when he realized he was still on the same page of his book as when he sat down. He had been quietly listening to the exchange the whole time and had not read a single word on the pages before him.

"I'm sure we can find some place for you to work here in the village. I think my old apartment is still empty, you can live there. It's small but-"

Naozumi grunted as she gave him a hug that almost took his breath away. "Thank you so much! That will be so freaking awesome!"

He laughed and stepped away from her, "I'm glad that it makes you happy." He went to his desk and opened a couple of drawers before stopping at the last one. He pulled out a small money bag and tossed it to her. "It isn't much, but it should cover you if you're careful with it until you get your first paycheck."

Raven gave him a grateful smile, "Thank you so much. I am so honored to have met you."

Naozumi looked at his sensei who still appeared to be engrossed in his book. He wasn't buying it. He had not seen him turn a single page since he had sat down. He was not sure what his sensei was about, but he was intentionally acting like he was bored to be there.

"Kioshi Sensei, since you've brought her this far could you please show her how to get to my old place?"

He lowered his book and gave a sigh, "If I must."

"When you're done, I have a few things to discuss with you about some things coming up."

"Right," he answered as he stood and shoved his book in his pack. "Come along, Raven. We've taken enough of his time."

Raven gave him a quick bow and smile before following Kioshi out the door. Naozumi crossed his arms in front of himself wondering what that was all about. He would find out soon enough when Kioshi got back. He liked Raven. Once he got news that she was settled, he would mention to Hikari that they should have her over for dinner. His wife would take to her immediately too. Her enthusiasm was contagious.

Raven looked at the apartment with some wonder. It was really run down and had collected a lot of dirt and grime since Naozumi had moved out. It still thrilled her to no end. She looked back at Kioshi who was standing silently at the door with his hands shoved into his pockets. He was completely unreadable.

"Thank you, Kioshi," she finally said. "I hope that I will see you around sometime."

"It's always a possibility," he responded before backing away. "Welcome to the wind village, Raven."

She watched him go and winced inwardly. She had a feeling that it would be a long while before she saw him again. She set Butter down and shut the door behind her, leaning against it. Here she finally was where she could not only see but touch Kioshi and she still couldn't break that barrier.

It sucked the enthusiasm out of her.

"Damn, he's even hotter in person Butter," she muttered. "And... he's just as far out of my reach as ever. I feel like the nerd that has a crush on the popular kid." She groaned and pushed away from the door. "Let's see if this place has any cleaning materials."

After looking in every cabinet, she discerned that there were no cleaning supplies. She found an old blanket and made a spot for Butter to sleep while she was gone. She was going to have to go shopping any ways. She had been pleased to see a washing machine, refrigerator, and a modern stove. At least that much of her life would be the same.

She locked the door and went downstairs. She did not venture very far, scared that she would get lost and not find her way back. The village was larger than she realized. She was careful to make note of landmarks to get back to her new home.

She found a shop a few blocks away that seemed to have everything she would need. Along with the cleaning supplies, she bought new sheets, a couple of changes of clothes, and a pair of sandals. The store clerk was very helpful and explained the value of each monetary item.

On the way back, she stopped at another shop and bought some cheap food staples. She wanted so bad to go to the ramen shop but until she was working and getting paid, she did not dare spend the money she had been given frivolously.

She was winded by the time she got back to the apartment with her arms loaded down. She set the items down on the kitchen counter and took her hoodie off. She pulled her phone out of her hoodie pocket and wondered if the charger would work in the outlets there.

She cringed, deciding not to even try it until the phone was almost dead. She knew she would never use it again to talk to anyone, but it did have precious photos of Leia, Riley, her family and friends. It also had her favorite songs downloaded on it. All of which was irreplaceable now that she was in this world.

Raven went to her favorite playlist for cleaning, turned the volume up as loud as the phone would go, then started the long process of scrubbing the apartment from top to bottom.

Kioshi stood silently in front of Naozumi after dropping off Raven. The younger man was looking at him his blue eyes narrowed on him. "Care to explain yourself?"

"Whatever do you mean, Naozumi?"

"The other day you were pretty wound up about this woman. Today she's here and you act like you are having an ordinary day. She literally knows everything about you, me, and most of the village."

Kioshi shrugged, "Just keeping myself uninvolved. Now that she is here, I won't be having those dreams anymore."

"You can't keep yourself completely uninvolved, Kioshi," he muttered with a sigh. "The ancients... universe... whatever has assigned you with the task of keeping an eye on her."

Kioshi shrugged, "If you say so."

"Okay, let me put it this way. I'm asking you to keep an eye on her." Naozumi finally said.

Kioshi frowned at him, "Why? She will be just fine. As you said, she knows everything about this place. You're meddling where you shouldn't meddle."

Naozumi narrowed his eyes on him then suddenly started laughing in understanding. "Now I understand."

Kioshi was irritated, "What do you understand?"

45

"You like her, and it scares the hell out of you."

Kioshi crossed his arms in front of him and looked away, "As I said, you're meddling where you shouldn't meddle, Naozumi."

Naozumi laughed a long while, wiping tears of laughter from his eyes. "I haven't been this interested since we tried to see under that mask of yours."

"May I remind you what the end result of that was?"

"We still have hopes of getting a peak," Naozumi countered. "This will be more interesting to watch. Very well, I won't order you to keep tabs on her, but I don't think I need to. You're not going to be able to help yourself."

Kioshi gave a quick nod of his head, "Thank you. Well I am off. I'm in the middle of a good book and my students are expecting me in the morning."

Chapter Four

Raven was beginning to get discouraged as she had yet to find one place that needed help. She was going to have to head back to the apartment soon to take Butter out. She had been gone most of the morning. Her stomach rumbled as the most delicious smell greeted her nose.

It was that ramen place. Of course.

She bit her lower lip, wanting so badly to go in but she knew she couldn't. She had worn the only dress she had purchased, hoping that it would make her appear more reliable to any potential employers.

She was about to pass the restaurant when she caught sight of the sign on the counter. She stopped and stared at it. She could not read it, but she wondered if it was a help wanted sign. She was going to look stupid if it wasn't. It was so strange that she could hear and understand, even speak the language but she could not read it. That was a bit frustrating. She was going to have to learn it or appear forever ignorant.

Raven straightened her shoulders and walked up to the counter. The young woman behind the counter she recognized from the show, but she could not for the life of her remember what her name was now. She gave her a big smile.

"Hi, I was wondering about the sign..."

"Oh, you're looking for a job?"

"Yes," Raven said in relief that it was a help wanted sign. "I am willing to do whatever the position requires. I'm a hard worker and will even let you test me out on trial without pay if you'll give me a chance."

She laughed, "That sounds good, but it is my father who will make the decision. Our restaurant has been expanding since Naozumi has become the Lord over the village. Everyone knows this is his favorite restaurant. We need extra hands serving, cleaning, and even cooking when necessary."

"I can do all that, but I will need to watch first the cooking as I've never made this fancy of ramen before. I've always had the instant."

The young woman laughed, "Oh you must try some. Here is a bowl on the house. Enjoy that while I go get my father."

Raven thanked her and drank in the smell of the ramen. It looked as good as it smelled. She picked up a set of chopsticks and eagerly started eating it. She felt like she had died and gone to heaven. It was so delicious. She had finished the bowl before the young woman had returned with her father.

"So, you want to work here do you?"

"Yes, sir! My name is Raven," She said as she came to her feet extending her hand in greeting. "I promise that I will work hard and not cut any corners. I will learn everything I need to learn."

"That's quite a promise," he said while nodding. "I'll give you a chance. Be here tomorrow at five in the morning to help open up shop."

"Thank you so much!" she exclaimed. "I'll see you tomorrow morning!"

Raven hurried down the street back to her apartment. She was so excited she could barely contain herself. She was so excited in fact that she collided with someone coming out of one of the shops. They went toppling to the ground in a flurry of arms and legs. She ended up on top as they turned so that they would take the brunt of the fall.

She pushed up in horror, "Oh my god, I'm so..."

Kioshi raised a brow at her from his sprawled position on the ground. His book that he had been reading instead of paying attention to where he was going was laying in the dirt to her left. "Well hello Raven," he said in a bored tone.

She felt her face turn ten shades of red as she looked down at him, "I'm so sorry Kioshi!" She reached over to pluck the book up out of the dirt.

Kioshi almost died as her breast literally slapped him in the face as she grabbed the book. She was completely unaware as she leaned back while sitting up, straddling him for a moment. She was wearing a dress and there was not a lot of material between them for that second in time. It was a moment in heaven and hell all at once. She then seemed to realize that was not a good position and shimmied off him to the side.

He sat up, his own face a little red as they had made quite a commotion in the middle of

49

the street. She was staring at the book when he looked over at her, her eyes were wide as she looked at the page. He snagged the book out of her hands, feeling his cheeks get even warmer. She laughed hard, holding her stomach.

"Oh my.... Well, I see why you were so... engrossed."

Raven had not been able to read the words in the book but the illustrations... She knew that he read naughty books, everyone that watched the show knew that, but that was a bit more than she had expected. If the illustrations were that graphic, she could just imagine what the words said.

"Kioshi, you're priceless," she said as she got to her feet. She extended her hand to assist him and he ignored it, immediately springing to his feet on his own volition. He dusted himself off and gave her a bored expression. He shoved one hand in his pocket while the other brought the book up to eye level once more.

"Have a nice day, Raven," he muttered.

Oh, he was in a mood. She chuckled and shook her head as she watched him walk away. "So that's the way of it, huh? Well good thing then because you couldn't handle me." She muttered with a forced laugh before starting back off towards her place again.

His attitude had smarted a bit. He was avoiding her and that did hurt. She knew him well enough to see the signs. He had literally done it to several people in the show. She shrugged, what did she expect? It did not mean it didn't hurt but she was in too good of a mood to let it sour because he was being himself. She had a job!

She bounded up the stairs to her place. She chuckled as she remembered the book again as she fished the key out of her pocket. She opened the door, was only two steps in before it slammed shut behind her, she was pushed back against it. In an instant she found herself pinned between a hunk of flesh and the door.

Raven stared into those dark gray eyes that had the most intense look she had ever seen leveled her way. She felt a chill go down her spine because it was a look she had only seen him give villains in the show. His left hand was braced against the door next to her head, while the right hand was still casually in his right pocket.

And how the hell did he get in here so fast after going in the opposite direction?

"I can't handle you. Did I hear you say that correctly?" He still had a bored inflection to his tone, but she could tell by the look in his eyes he was anything but bored. He was furious.

Raven bit her lower lip nervously and was having a hard time maintaining eye contact with him. He was so intense it made her insides flutter. "I didn't think you heard that."

His eyes narrowed slightly, "So you admit to saying it?"

She crossed her arms in front of her and narrowed her eyes back at him. She knew him well enough to know he wasn't going to hurt her in any way. He was trying to bully her, and it wasn't going to work.

"Yes, I did say it," she responded while lifting her chin up defiantly and narrowed her eyes back at him in what she hoped was an intimidating glare. "I meant every word of it too."

Okay, that part was a lie. She was blustering now, her pride smarting from his earlier rejection. She could not help but hit him in his own pride.

His eyes crinkled at the sides as he leaned back, lowering his hand for a moment. It was a strange look of humor mixed with anger. He slowly peeled off one of his gloves, then the other. He shoved them in his pack at his hip with a calculated calm. What was he up to now? He tilted his head to the side before his left palm slammed into the door to the right of her head, then his right palm slammed to the left. She flinched but managed to not break eye contact with him.

He leaned in towards her, close enough that she could see the faint outline of his lips beneath the mask. They were kicked up in a smile that did not reach his eyes.

"I think that we should put that to the test," Kioshi said with a sarcastic inflection of tone. "What do you say?"

Raven felt her mouth drop open at the words. Surely he did not mean what it sounded like he meant.

He moved so fast that she did not even have time to prepare herself. His left hand went up into her hair, holding her head in place as the right hand quickly lowered his mask before he crushed her lips beneath his own. She did not even have time to see his face it happened so quickly.

Raven gasped giving him just the opportunity to bring his tongue into play as he crushed her against the door. His lips and tongue moved in such a way that she was quickly lost beneath the onslaught. He was a master at kissing, employing a variety of movements from gentle biting to exploration that made her legs go weak. Her long pent up emotions towards him made resistance of any kind impossible.

Kioshi had meant to teach her a lesson about mouthing off like she had done. Knowing that she secretly had a crush on him was his weapon of choice, it being an obvious means to subdue her. Especially after what she had said. When he heard her muttered words, anger like he had not felt in a very long time had risen in him. It was like getting a cut to his manhood, insinuating he was not man enough for her. He had doubled back fast, taking the rooftops to save time. It had been nothing to pick the lock on the balcony door and enter her apartment to wait.

Now as he was pressing against her soft body and tasting her so completely, he was getting a lesson himself in losing self-control. His manhood was hard as a rock, painfully so. He did not realize how quickly that could happen just from kissing. He was a man that read erotica casually, so it was quite a shock for him as he felt his own self-control slipping.

He forced himself to pull away from her. Her eyes were closed, and she looked like she was about to melt. He could not stop his satisfied grin. It rather pleased him that he had done that to her after a relatively short kiss.

"I think I have made my point," he responded, purposefully making his voice sound bored as he pulled his mask back up.

Raven gasped at the words, her eyes flying open. They were now a shade of green, the brown almost completely gone. He turned away from her before she could see how she had affected him. He reached into his pack and pulled his gloves back on as he walked to the balcony.

"By the way, your dog is not much of an alarm. She didn't even bark when I came in."

Raven was still angry when she woke up very early the next morning. She could have slugged the arrogant ass. Worst yet, she had enjoyed the kiss that had been nothing more than a means of putting her in her place. He had made it quite clear that he could take advantage of her at any time but had no desire to do so. She did not have much of an ego but that tiny little bit of hope that she had clung to had been crushed. It was painful. So painful that it made her mad that he had to go out of his way to crush it.

She punched her pillow before getting up. She was so tired. Her sleep had been fitful because of that man. She went into the bathroom and took a quick shower. She skipped washing her hair because she had done so the night before. She pulled her hair up into a quick ponytail before dressing in the very simple pants and top she had bought.

Raven left the bathroom and grabbed her tennis shoes. She pulled them on then looked at Butter as she grabbed her leash and harness. The little dog gave a long stretch before coming over to her, obviously sleepy. It was only three forty-five in the morning after all.

Since she was due at the restaurant at five, she had to get up at three thirty so that she could take a bath, take Butter for a walk, and eat before going. Raven hesitated as she picked up her ankle holster with her gun. She doubted that she needed it in the Wind Village but what if she came across some kind of wild animal while walking Butter.

She strapped it on, hiding it once more beneath her pants before taking the leash and tugging her sleepy pet towards the door. It would take them a while to get used to the early morning routine, but they would.

Raven put her hoodie on next, zipping it up. The mornings in the Wind Village had been chilly since she arrived. She wondered if it would snow there in the winter. She tried to remember if she ever saw an episode with snow, but she could not remember if she had or not. Details such as that was not something that stuck in her mind.

She looked at the charge level still on her phone. She had a little more time before she would have to try plugging it in. She sighed, knowing no amount of conservation was going to alter the inevitable. She plugged her headphones

in, popped them into her ears, then tugged Butter
to the door.

The songs made her feel better as they
made their way through the empty streets. Only
the occasional patrol crossed their path but
thankfully they did not detain her, taking note of
the little dog at her side. Eventually they would
recognize her face and she would not even be a
blip on their radar.

It took about five minutes from her place
to get to the closest open field that ran parallel
with a cluster of trees. It was the perfect place for
Butter to do her business. In the early hour, she
did not have to worry about encountering anyone
else. Raven unlatched the leash, releasing her to
explore.

"Go potty, Butter," she said softly,
wrapping her arms around herself against the
chill.

The little dog immediately went off but
not out of Raven's view. She yawned as she
watched her, she really could have killed Kioshi
for disturbing her mind so much. Her first day
and she was going to be fighting exhaustion the
entire time.

She closed her eyes as one of her favorite
song began to play in her ear. She absently
started singing along to it as she swayed in tune to
the beat.

*"Well, you only need the light when it's
burning low, only miss the sun when it starts to
snow, only know you love her when you let her
go. Only know you've been high when you're
feeling low, only hate the road when you're*

missing home, only know you love her when you let her go."

Butter started barking like crazy and Raven came immediately back to the present. Someone grabbed her from behind, lifting her completely off her feet. She cursed and reared her head back, trying to head butt them in the nose.

Whoever it was, they smelled awful. Butter charged but was kicked hard and flung across the open field. Raven immediately went limp to throw them off by her sudden dead weight. It worked and they stumbled as they tried to readjust to the change in weight.

As she slipped in their grasp, she reared her arm back and elbowed them in the crotch. Over the music blaring in her ears, she heard a howl as they released her. She toppled to the ground and scrambled to put some distance between them while going for her gun at the same time. The headphones were jostled out of her ears.

Raven turned as she heard them coming at her. She steadied her arms and fired, just as Mark had shown her how to fire a weapon. The gun's blast was exceptionally loud in the silence.

She watched as the burly man's head snapped back and he fell to the ground with a loud thud. She was stunned and sat staring at his lifeless form for a long time.

Rapidly approaching footsteps came up behind her and she jerked in response, raising the weapon up for round two. Wood instantly surrounded her hands and the weapon, rendering them useless. She was shocked as vines appeared out of nowhere and wrapped around her, trapping her before she could even begin to fight.

"Don't move," a masculine voice stated before passing her to look at the man she had shot.

She was stunned as she looked between him and the block of wood that had formed around her hands and gun. She knew there was only one person who could do that, Yoshiaki. One of Kioshi's comrades and friends from the days when he was in the Shadow unit.

"He's dead," Yoshiaki stated before turning to look at her with a stoic expression that revealed nothing that he was thinking. "Are you going to use your weapon on me if I release you?"

Raven shook her head negative, feeling stunned that she had killed a man. When she was firing, she had been in full fight mode. She could feel a tremor go through her as the adrenaline was beginning to subside. In that same moment the vines unwrapped from around her and the block of wood retreated. She lowered her gun and put it back in the holster on her ankle. She was shaking noticeably by then and had a hard time getting it back in.

Yoshiaki came to her side carrying Butter. "This is your animal?"

Raven felt her eyes burn as she heard Butter crying. "Yes, she tried to help me." She took Butter from his arms and buried her face into her soft fur. After a moment Butter stopped whining.

"She is uninjured, just scared," he responded to her relief. "He must have been a rogue Ninja; his headband is from the land of earth. Are you injured?"

"No.... I've never killed anyone before."

Yoshiaki met her eyes in the dark. She was surprised at what he looked like in comparison to the anime. The overall details were the same, dark hair and eyes with light colored skin. However, on the show his features were rather dull and flat. He was handsome and that did surprise her. His eyes were almond shaped but large, with thick lashes that a girl would kill for. They were his most prominent feature. His nose was perfectly proportioned on his face, while his lips were full.

"I saw him coming up behind you, but you took care of him before I could reach you," he stated bluntly. "I apologize for restraining you; however, I did not think you would know friend from foe at that moment."

Raven smiled for the first time, "You are right. I was ready to shoot you too."

An awkward silence followed the statement.

"You sing nice," he then stated, and she was glad it was dark because she could feel her cheeks warm. "However, I would advise to be more aware if you are going to go out this early in the morning. We are at peace but there are still individuals like him looking for easy marks."

"You were following me?"

Yoshiaki smiled slightly, "Yes. I saw you in town and thought you might get into trouble."

Raven laughed, "I look like a troublemaker to you?"

"No, but those of us on patrol duty was advised of your arrival to the village. I thought you might not be as cautious as one of the locals, so I followed you. My instincts were correct." He looked at where she had put her gun. "What kind of weapon did you use? The back of his head is gone."

"It's called a gun. My model is a .380. I had it on me for personal protection when I was brought to this world," she answered.

"Can you stand? You should return to the village."

"I think so," she answered while getting to her feet.

"Were you listening to music?" he asked as they started walking back to the village. "How?"

Raven grinned at him and pulled her phone out of her pocket. She switched the song back to the one she had been listening to before handing one of the headphones to him.

"Put it up to your ear," she instructed.

He hesitated for a moment before doing so. His eyes widened slightly, and he pulled it back to look at it once again then replaced it to his ear again. He smiled as he listened.

"I like that song," he stated before reluctantly handing the headphone back to her.

"This is called a phone. In my world, we use it to talk to people great distances away. We can store music on it like you just heard. We can also watch shows and look up information on it."

His dark brows were raised, "That is a very handy device."

"Yes and no," she responded.

"Explain."

"People in my world are very distracted by them. It has kind of affected our interaction with each other in person. We are more comfortable talking through these than to each other. You can be in the same room with someone and not even greet each other."

"Hmm," he responded. "I see."

"Thank you for watching out for me."

He gave her a big smile, "It is part of my duties. I am Yoshiaki. Your name is Raven, correct?"

Raven smiled back at him, "Yes." She looked back to where they had left. "What about him?"

"Someone will collect and dispose of him," Yoshiaki replied. "Do not worry about it. Are you doing anything today?"

Raven blinked at the question. "I have to be at work at five. It is why I am out so early today. I start at Itsuki's restaurant today."

"Would you be willing to go to dinner with me afterwards?" Yoshiaki asked with a smile.

"Like a date?"

He laughed, "Yes, you can call it that. I am curious about you and where you came from."

Raven felt her face warm a little. Kioshi's image came to her mind and she shoved it away.

He had made his feelings more than clear. "Okay, that would be nice."

They had just returned to the brightly lit streets. The village was starting to come alive. "I will meet you outside Itsuki's when you are done."

"I'm looking forward to it," she smiled.

Yoshiaki smiled then disappeared from her view as he went back on patrol. She was amazed at how fast he moved, so much like Kioshi.

Raven looked to the sky, noting that it was getting lighter. She quickly hurried back to her place, dropped Butter off and ate something fast before hurrying out the door. The last thing she wanted was to be late on her first day.

Chapter Five

Kioshi was reading his book while walking home from the Academy. He was having a hard time focusing on it, which was annoying. It was Raven's fault he was so distracted. He had been mildly aroused ever since kissing her yesterday. He had gone straight home to relieve himself in a hot shower after teaching her a lesson.

He had to admit, he was attracted to her. Even more so after sharing that kiss with her. He gave a heavy sigh. He just had to stay away from her, eventually it would go away and he could go back to fully enjoying his books and solitude. He could not give her what she would want in any case and it was better he kept her at arm's length. Not just for himself but also for her.

He glanced up when he heard someone humming a tune that he did not recognize. He could not contain his surprise as he saw his old friend, Yoshiaki, standing in front of a store using his reflection in the glass to adjust his shirt and run his hands nervously through his hair.

Kioshi almost laughed. He had never seen him in anything but his patrol clothes. Even on his days off, he wore the same gear, always ready. To see him somewhat dressed up was a surprised. As he came closer, the strong smell of cologne hit him and he could not help himself, he had to ask.

"Yoshiaki," he greeted him while lowering his book.

The younger man glanced over at him and then grinned, "Kioshi, how are you?"

They were not that much different in age, five years at best with Yoshiaki being the younger. They had never actually talked about age, but they had served long enough together it was a good guess.

"I am well," he responded. "You are all dressed up. What is the occasion?"

Yoshiaki grinned at him, "I have a date."

Kioshi raised both brows and lowered the book completely to his side, "Well that is an unusual development." He smiled beneath his mask, good for him. "Who is the lady?"

Yoshiaki's gave him a smug smile, "Raven."

Kioshi was stunned but managed to keep it from his expression. He shoved his book into his pack before crossing his arms in front of him. "Really? That is a surprise. When did you meet her?"

"This morning while on patrol," Yoshiaki responded.

Kioshi stilled, "I heard something about a rogue ninja attacking someone outside of town. It was her?"

"Yes, but she handled him on her own," Yoshiaki chuckled. "Fierce little thing when she needs to be. She was shaken up after, apparently the first person she's ever killed. I escorted her back and asked her out."

"Isn't she a little bit too old for you," Kioshi asked after a moment of silence.

Yoshiaki raised his brows at Kioshi. The look on the other man's face was dark. He remembered that it was Kioshi that had found and brought her to the village. He almost laughed at the question.

"I don't know, honestly," he responded. "She looks pretty young to me. If she is older it isn't by enough to dissuade me."

"I am a little surprised, Yoshiaki," Kioshi said in a tone that sounded bored, but Yoshiaki knew better. "She's not someone I thought you would be interested in."

"Why wouldn't I be interested? She's pretty, especially when she smiles. She's got fight in her which is important when selecting a mate. I'm also very curious about where she came from."

If Kioshi had been drinking anything he would have choked. "When selecting a mate?"

The other man gave him a nod, "I have been thinking for a while now that I would like to have a family. Now that we are at peace with the other nations, it is a good time for that. I read a book that gives some outlines on finding the right mate."

"You read a book..."

"Hey, I don't mean to ditch you, but I have to get to Itsuki's. She'll be getting off work soon and I told her I would pick her up then. See you later, Kioshi."

Kioshi watched as he disappeared down the street to the restaurant a few blocks away. So, she was working at Itsuki's. He shoved his hands into his pockets. Yoshiaki was a good man; he should be happy for her. Yes, his background was... unusual but he had overcome his upbringing remarkably well. He had a strange sense of humor sometimes and had creeped out Naozumi several times with that sense of humor. He had a feeling that Raven would find that off beat sense of humor hilarious.

Yoshiaki was ready and willing to give her what she ultimately needed. A home, children possibly, stability. It would also get any temptation from her locked away permanently. Kioshi should have been happy about the solution to his problem.

So why did it make him want to grab Yoshiaki and throttle him?

Raven was impressed at how handsome Yoshiaki was when he dressed up. He was achingly cute as he fidgeted with his hair and the buttons at his throat in his nervousness. She could see him as a little boy. On the show, he had been so cute with those big eyes. Like many of the characters, his growing years had been traumatic, and he was the product of human experimentation.

Yet his spirit has always been rather sweet on the show. Clueless as he had been learning and growing after being set free, but he was exceptionally sweet. She wished that she had asked him to pick her up at her place after she got a chance to change and dress up as well.

Her feet were killing her from standing most of the day. It had been hard work, a large portion of it spent cleaning up behind everyone else. Yet she felt good about working hard with her hands and body.

"You look very nice, Yoshiaki," she said with a smile to reassure him. "Would you mind if we go back to my place really quick so I can get out of these dirty clothes?"

"Oh, absolutely," he said with a smile.

Raven started that way then was surprised when he took her hand, a bit awkwardly, before matching her pace. He smiled at her and she almost laughed. He looked rather pleased.

"How was work? Did you like what you were doing?"

"It was very busy," she responded with a grin. "But I did like it. I'm glad that they are giving me a chance. There is something very satisfying in working with your hands."

He gave a nod to her response, "Yes, it makes you feel like you have earned your pay."

"Exactly," she grinned at him. "I really like Itsuki too. I have a lot of respect for him."

Kioshi scowled as he watched Raven and Yoshiaki enter her apartment building from his perch on the neighboring building. The building had a nice view of the city and a gazebo on top that was perfect for relaxation. His book was long forgotten in his lap. He had come to the spot for privacy, he had told himself. That it happened to overlook her apartment was just coincidence.

He forced himself to pick his book back up. The words swam in front of his eyes as he tried to read it. He kept setting it down to look towards the apartment. He finally gave up and scowled in its general direction.

Why were they taking so long?

He was about to get up and investigate when they finally left the building again. Yoshiaki had wasted no time and was holding her hand in his.

Kioshi frowned as he looked at Raven. She was wearing a red dress that really complemented her skin and hair. He did not care for how closely it fit her, though. It was snug across her breasts, emphasizing them with the material gathering just under them before flaring out in a free-flowing style. He scowled even deeper as he saw the top swells of her breasts and a small amount of cleavage as the neckline dipped a little low. Nothing that was inappropriate really, but it infuriated him to no end.

Kioshi saw red when Yoshiaki abruptly pulled her up along his side and wrapped his arm across her shoulders in a rather possessive fashion. He angrily tossed his book down to the ground in response.

Raven looked up in surprise at Yoshiaki. She had not expected him to be so forward. He smiled at her, "I'm new to all this so let me know if I'm doing something wrong."

She grinned at him, "Is this your first date?"

"Yes," he responded. "Is that strange to you?"

"Not really," she replied. "Y'all have been at war a long time. I imagine there really hasn't been much of a chance for anything else."

Yoshiaki smiled at her response. He had caught sight of Kioshi earlier while waiting on her by the balcony in the apartment. His suspicions from earlier had been correct. Kioshi was interested in her whether he wanted to admit it or not. It was quite humorous. He was obviously trying to fight what he was feeling, or he would not have acted like it was nothing earlier. His act of possession was for Kioshi's benefit.

He knew the man well enough to know he would be stubborn about getting into a relationship. He signed inwardly, though. He had hoped that maybe Raven was the one for him but now that he knew Kioshi had already laid claim to her, there was no way he could earnestly pursue her.

He hoped that if he could help make Kioshi jealous enough to act on what he really wanted; it would help his friend. It might cause him to get beat up, but it would be worth it if Kioshi found some happiness at last.

"What did you do in your world?"

"I worked at a jail," she responded. "A place where we locked up criminals. My job was to watch their visits with outsiders and make sure the rules were observed."

He raised his brows, "Is that where you learned how to use your... gun?"

Raven smiled at him; her eyes were rather dark at that moment. Damn that Kioshi. She really was pretty when she smiled.

"No, my best friend Mark taught me
after my husband died," she replied.

"You were married?" he asked in
surprise.

"Yes, for ten years."

"No children?"

Raven got a sad look on her face, "Yes,
we had a daughter. She died when she was two
years old from a medical condition. My husband
never fully recovered from her death, so when he
got sick, he didn't fight it."

"I'm sorry," Yoshiaki responded. He
wondered if Kioshi knew any of that. "I have
seen that happen when a child dies suddenly."
He cleared his throat, "Ah, here's the restaurant.
I have heard others talk about bringing their dates
here."

Raven smiled at him and he was relieved
to see she was distracted from the previous
conversation.

When they went inside, he lowered his
arm. The hostess took them to a booth in the
back. He watched Raven and had to laugh at the
expression of excitement in her eyes. It was like
watching a child experiencing something for the
very first time as she eyed the cooking rack in the
center of the table.

"Do you want me to order?"

"Yes," she grinned. "I'm not sure what
I'd like."

He looked to the hostess, "Some pork
and chicken, I think, and some rice balls. Oh,
and some dumplings after we've finished."

"To drink?"

"Green tea and a bottle of Sake?"

"Very good," she responded before leaving. She returned a moment later with some uncooked meat, a tray of 3 rice balls, and what looked like a couple donuts on a stick. She then poured them each a cup of hot tea and set a medium sized bottle with two small cups down next to Yoshiaki. "Is there anything else?"

"No, this will do," he responded.

Raven smiled as he explained what everything was and showed her how they would cook. At one point he leaned forward and the light of the fire cast a shadow across his face, and he made a spooky face at her. She laughed hard. He was quite the comedian. He kept her well entertained through the meal.

Yoshiaki handed her a small glass as he poured the sake for her, "This is rather strong so I would suggest not drinking very much unless you want to act foolish."

She laughed, "I'm more curious as to how it will taste. I've never had sake. We have it in my world too, but I've never tasted it."

"You will either love it or hate it," he declared.

She eyed it for a moment before straightening her shoulders, "Here goes."

He laughed at the look that crossed her face as she drank the first glass, "You hate it."

"It's like kerosene," she wheezed.

Yoshiaki laughed before offering one of the sticks of dumplings to her, "I know you will like this better."

Raven had a great time with Yoshiaki, but she honestly was not having that strong of a romantic attraction with him. He was so funny and charming, but she was having a hard time seeing him as anything more than a friend. He was resting his arm across her shoulder again.

"When is your next day off?"

"Day after tomorrow."

"Would you come with me to the park? I will bring food and drinks. We can just relax and talk." He leaned down close to her, "Just as friends if you like."

She blinked as she looked up at him then laughed, "Ah, so you felt that, too did you?"

"Unfortunately," he sighed heavily. "But we can be very good friends, I think. I haven't had any friends that are girls before so I think there is a lot I could learn from you. Maybe you can even help me find, the one."

Raven laughed, "Absolutely. You're very charming, I'm sure there is someone out there just perfect for you. And, yes, I will come with you to the park."

"Excellent," he responded before stopping in front of her apartment complex. "I'll see you then around eight. We can spend the day out and you can bring Butter with you."

"That sounds like fun," she responded.

He surprised her once more when he leaned forward and kissed her forehead. "See you then, Raven."

Raven smiled as he walked off down the street. She had a feeling she was going to have a great friendship with him. He was such a

sweetheart of a guy. She would have to keep her
eyes open for a girl as sweet as him.

Yoshiaki whistled as he strolled down the
street to his home. He had sensed he was being
followed the minute he had left Raven's place.
He barely restrained his laughter, even though he
was probably going to get his new outfit ruined.
All the hands on had done exactly what he had
hoped. The forehead kiss at the end was just the
icing on the cake. He was not surprised when the
presence behind him ended. Most likely he
would have to duck the moment he stepped into
his apartment.

He was a little disappointed when he
unlocked his door, stepped inside, and nothing
happened. At least, not what he had expected to
happen. As he turned the light on, he saw
Kioshi's shape sitting on the railing outside on his
balcony. His hands were folded in front of him,
as if he was preparing for battle.

Yoshiaki took the unexpected moment
to pull off his dress shirt and then pull on a tank
top instead. He opened the balcony door and
stood silent, looking at his friend.

"Hey Kioshi, what are you doing here?"

Kioshi had wanted to pound him into the
ground only a few moments before but as he sat
on the railing, he knew he could not do that to
his friend. As much as his blood was boiling, he
could not do that. He had the suspicion that
Yoshiaki had known he was following him by the
way he had looked around his apartment
surprised. He almost laughed when he saw him

notice him on the balcony. He had taken the time to change his shirt in the event things got physical.

"Somehow I think you are not surprised I am here," he finally responded to the question.

Yoshiaki laughed, "So you are interested in her."

Kioshi glared at him, "I didn't say that."

"Your presence here does," he remarked. "You have no reason to come here otherwise. Unless there is some kind of mission?"

Kioshi heaved a heavy sigh, "I don't know why I am here to be truthful."

"You're jealous," he chuckled. "Even I can figure that one out, Kioshi."

"Are you going to keep seeing her?"

Yoshiaki gave him a smile that made his blood boil. "Absolutely. We have another date in a few days."

"Cancel it," Kioshi growled.

"Oh no, that is not how this works Kioshi," Yoshiaki stated. "If you were claiming her as your own, I would respectfully step back. That is not the case, though, is it?"

Kioshi narrowed his eyes on him.

"You're reading more into this," Kioshi finally said after a minute. "I just don't think the two of you would be suited to one another."

"We can figure that out for ourselves," Yoshiaki responded. "Is there anything else? I really need to get to sleep, I've got patrol in a few hours."

Kioshi wanted to smack him in the face but he was right. He had no claim over Raven. He felt foolish for even coming to his friend's place to demand he stop seeing her.

He gave him a sharp nod of his head and left.

Yoshiaki chuckled inwardly as his friend disappeared into the darkness. Another man would have backed down to Kioshi. He was formidable and intimidating but Yoshiaki had been his comrade and friend for many years. He was not intimidated by him as others would be.

It went exactly as he had planned. He was certain that when he took Raven to the park, Kioshi would be there. Most likely hiding but he would be there. He was torturing himself for no good reason. If he could make Kioshi jealous enough, he would finally act on what he wanted despite his fears.

Kioshi was frustrated as he pulled his shirt off. For the first time in many years, the home seemed too quiet, too empty. He could not believe how much she was affecting him. Was it just sexual frustration?

He had managed to avoid that pitfall for the entirety of his life until now. He stared at his image in the mirror for a long moment. Perhaps that was what he needed to do. Just bed her and get it over with. Surely that would get it out of his system.

He cursed and hit the wall. Yoshiaki had made that impossible now that he was dating her.

He could not bed the woman that his friend was courting.

"Damn it, Yoshiaki!"

Kioshi raked his fingers through his hair before dropping back onto his bed. He threw his arm over his eyes, unable to see any way out of his situation. He could not claim her as Yoshiaki was telling him to do. He was a harbinger of death. He would destroy her life and he could not do that to her. Everyone that he had ever cared deeply for had died. The blood on his hands was so thick that it was be blasphemy to put that blood on another.

An idea finally came to him after he allowed his mind to clear and refocus. "I'll ask Naozumi for a mission, a long one. By the time I get back, perhaps she'll be completely claimed, and I'll be able to let her go."

He gave a long, heavy sigh. Yes, that is what he would do.

Chapter Six

Raven tilted her head into the warm rays of the sun. It was a beautiful day to spend at the park. It was more of an open field that backed up to the trees than an actual park. They were not completely alone, though, either. In the distance, she could see other couples and families enjoying the location.

Butter was enjoying exploring the area around them but after a while had come back to lay near them. She really was a lazy dog.

They had already eaten lunch and now they were relaxing beneath a tree. Yoshiaki had stretched out a moment ago and put his head in her lap, looking very much like one about to take a nap. She shook her head and laughed at him.

"You know people will have the wrong idea about what is going on between us," she said softly.

"I don't mind, I'm practicing."

Raven laughed hard at the answer and hesitantly brushed one lock of hair from his forehead. He smiled at the action, "That was nice. Do it again."

"Now they definitely will get the wrong idea."

She grinned down at him but did as he requested, brushing his hair back with her fingers lightly. It was a rather peaceful experience. She leaned back against the tree and turned her eyes to the clouds drifting lazily by. His locks were soft, and it was relaxing stroking them.

"I honestly think you could become my very best friend here, Yoshiaki," she said softly. "I really hope you find a woman who will love you like you deserve."

He opened his dark eyes and smiled up at her, "Thank you, my dear. You're going to put me to sleep if you keep that up. I'm just warning you now."

She laughed, "So be it. I'm finding it very relaxing. You have really soft hair."

He chuckled and closed his eyes, "Don't say I didn't warn you when you're stuck here for a while."

Kioshi felt almost sick watching them from the tree he was perching in. He had told himself to stay away and avoid them until he left on mission in the morning. Instead he had found himself following them discretely until they reached the park. They looked like the perfect couple enjoying a perfect day. He kept telling himself to leave but he could not do it.

It was very clear that they were having a great time together. He wanted to punch Yoshiaki when he laid his head in her lap. Then he wanted to shake her when she started playing with his hair.

How could she so easily change her focus from him to Yoshiaki? Especially after that kiss he had laid on her that had almost done him in. It had done her in too. She was almost melted in his arms when he pulled away.

Kioshi was glaring at them without even realizing it. The look she had on her face as she

stared up to the clouds was the same expression
she used to have on her face when she was
watching his character on her TV. It made him
angry. He had not taken her for someone who
was that fickle. He clinched his hand at his side
before punching the tree.

Raven closed her eyes as she stroked
Yoshiaki's hair. In her mind, she was pretending
that it was Kioshi's hair. She had not seen him
since he had come to teach her a lesson. She had
been so furious with him but now she had to
admit that she had asked for it. She had
challenged his manhood and he had shown her
just how much he could melt her if he wanted to.
Granted, she had not planned on him hearing
her challenge. She had said it for her own
wounded pride not as a dig at him.
    She sighed and looked down at her
friend. That brat. He really did fall asleep on
her. She laughed as she looked at him, seeing
the little boy that had not had a chance to be a
child. He was precious. Her mind went to her
boss' daughter, who was single and sweet. She
wondered if the two of them would hit it off. She
would have to invite him to eat there and see if
there were any sparks.
    Raven gasped as Kioshi suddenly landed
right in front of her. He knelt to where he was at
eye level with her. He appeared to be smiling but
the feeling that she got from him was anything but
happiness.
    "Well what have we got here? You two
look rather cozy."

He then grabbed Yoshiaki by the front of his shirt and yanked him up abruptly. She gasped in shock as he then punched him hard before tossing him to the side.

"Kioshi, what the fuck?!" She yelled at him.

Raven gave a small shriek as he grabbed her up and tossed her over his shoulder like she was nothing.

Yoshiaki was laughed where he was sprawled on the grass while rubbing his jaw. "So, does this mean what I hope it means?"

"I suppose it does," Kioshi said.

"But did you have to hit me so damn hard?"

Kioshi narrowed his eyes on him but could not respond as Raven had started pounding on his back and yelling. The obscenities coming out of her mouth would leave a haze around the whole of the earth.

"Take care of Butter, please."

Raven screamed as he jumped up into the tree with her. She was beyond furious and if he thought for a minute he was going to just haul off with her, he had another thing coming. She bit him on the back and he almost dropped her. She jerked as his free hand gave her a hard swat on the butt in response.

"Damn you, Kioshi Hamasaki! Just what the hell are you doing?" She screamed.

He did not answer and that just made her angrier. The ground was moving past so quickly that her head was spinning. She gave him a few more hits that seemed to do absolutely nothing. He finally landed on the ground and she saw a narrow walkway pass before her eyes.

"Let me go you baboon!" she yelled and started hitting him again, doing her best to make as much noise as possible. "I swear I will never forgive you! I hate you!"

She heard a door slam open and then heard it slam behind them before she was unceremoniously dumped on a mat at his feet. The impact jarred her for a moment before she could react. He knelt in front of her.

His eyes were just as intense as the last time she had seen him. Even more so because he was clearly very angry. He was ripping off his gloves this time and throwing them carelessly to the side. She then gasped when he ripped his mask off and tossed his headband to the side.

Raven had suspected he was handsome, but this was excessive. She was momentarily stunned to see him. Then she remembered how he had punched her new best friend and then treated her like a piece of property in front of who knows how many people.

"You son of a bitch," she yelled before lunging at him while taking a swing at his face.

Kioshi grabbed her in mid-swing, flipped her legs out from under her and slammed her to the mat flat on her back. She shrieked but he had crushed her under him, easily pinning her. She knew she did not have a chance against him in a physical battle, but she was so angry she could not stop trying to get at least one good hit in.

It took her a moment to realize he was laughing.

"Enough Raven. You're only going to hurt yourself."

She gave one last screech before relaxing, her breath was coming in and out hard from her previous efforts. He had both of her wrists locked above her head inside one of his hands. His legs were on either side of her own, effectively trapping her lower body and with his left hand he propped himself up to look down at her. A satisfied smile was on his handsome face.

"I am glad you saw reason."

"I can't believe you did that to Yoshiaki!" she growled. "He's your friend. What in the hell were you thinking?"

His humor disappeared at her words and his dark eyes narrowed on her. The look he was giving her was one of dark anger. "I'll do the same to any man that touches what is mine."

Raven only has a moment to process what he was saying before he captured her lips in a punishing kiss. His anger and frustration were clear in the way he was kissing her. He broke the kiss to move his lips down her neck.

"I tried, Raven, I really tried to walk away from you. To ignore you. To spare you." He whispered. "But I just couldn't take watching you with someone else. You're mine, Raven. I won't share you with anyone, do you understand?"

Before she could say anything, he captured her lips once more, this time the kiss was different than before. It was sensual, thrilling and more like the kiss he had given her in her apartment. He was doing things to her lips that she had never experienced before, and it felt amazing.

"I'm going to make love to you right now," he whispered against her lips. "Don't you dare say no or fight this. I know how you feel about me, I saw it before you even came here. I am in agony because of my need for you."

Raven moaned as he teased her lips, allowing her time to speak. She opened her eyes to see he was staring at her. "I could never say no to you, Kioshi."

Those dark eyes gleamed at the answer and he pulled her up from the mat. He wrapped her legs around his hips as he walked with her to the bedroom. He was kissing her in that way that turned her to a quivering pile of flesh. He laid her down on his bed and once again covered her. His hands were all over her body and his mouth made love to her own. His teeth would occasionally chew her bottom lip then her top before his tongue would dance with her own before exploring every inch of her mouth.

He pulled back only briefly to pull her shirt over her head and remove her bra. He then leaned down and his lips captured first one nipple then the second, suckling deep each one. She gasped, unconsciously arching against him.

Kioshi could not believe he had managed to go all these years without giving into lust and it only took one woman to take his control and burn it to shreds. He could not help but have a bit of excitement, knowing he was about to experience firsthand the mysteries in his books.

He released her breast from his mouth and slid back. He hooked her pants and underwear in his fingers, pulling them off as he backed off the bed. She bit her lip, feeling very exposed and self-conscious of her body under his gaze. He quickly discarded his utility pack, unbuttoned his pants, and removed them from his body.

She stared transfixed at his body and the instrument of his manhood. It was huge, bigger than she could have ever imagined. He knelt at the end of the bed, parting her legs. She was not prepared as he spread her thighs before pressing his mouth against her core. She almost came up off the bed. That was something that Riley had never done to her.

"Oh my god, Kioshi!"

She wrapped her fingers through his silver hair, amazed at how soft it was to the touch. He held her hips down firmly as he had his fill of her, not letting up until her first release was upon her. Raven felt completely ravished. His lips trailed back up her body, nipping and licking all the way. His hips nudged her thighs apart to accommodate him between them.

Kioshi could still taste her and he felt intoxicated. He was so aroused that it was painful. He was going to have to get inside her soon or he would embarrass himself by releasing on her thigh instead of inside her. He gently was probing against her wetness with the head of his cock. He released her breast to slide his hand down between them. She groaned as she felt his long finger slide between her lower lips, testing her and finding her entrance.

Raven's eyes widened as she felt his very ridged cock replace the finger and begin to probe her lightly, hesitantly. His lips were against her neck, biting and licking. She realized that he was not sure how to proceed as his movements were testing. He had to be in agony.

Kioshi kissed her feverishly as she suddenly reached between them to help guide him to the right spot. When he felt her flesh give way a little he knew to press forward and made a loud grunt as he sunk himself to the hilt inside of her. He groaned, she was so tight and squeezed him in a way that the books never could have prepared him for.

Raven gasped too at how full and deep he had gone inside her due to his massive size. It was an incredible feeling to be so full. He began moving inside of her and she gasped at how easily they fell into the perfect rhythm.

His lips went back to her neck, sucking and nipping on it while whispering dirty between each kiss and nip. His words were making her even more excited as did each groan, grunt, and moan that came from his mouth. Knowing he had never done it before made the experience even more exhilarating. She was crying out and saying all kinds of things as he brought her up to a point that was beyond anything she had ever experienced, even in her ten years of marriage.

Raven cried out as her orgasm roared over her, drowning out everything. She vaguely heard herself saying his name repeatedly as he continued to slam into her, his pace becoming faster as he reached his limit.

Kioshi stiffened as his pleasure reached its peak and his seed poured out of him. He cried out while still pumping into her until the last drop left him. It was a feeling so incredible the books he had read did not do it justice. He collapsed on top of her as his energy was spent.

His body felt like it was having small tremors rolling through it. He could feel her heartbeat against his chest and her legs were shaking. As his body started coming back under his control, he had instant concern that he might have hurt her. He was not sure he was that gentle when he thrust into her. That moment had been something he would never forget. Her sheath had encased him tightly. It had been warm and wet, feeling more incredible than he could have ever imagined as it clasped him and pulled him in deep.

Kioshi slowly raised his head to look down at her. His breathing was still labored but he had to know she was okay. She had a dazed look on her face. "Raven, are you okay? Did I hurt you? I'm sorry, I did not know for sure..."

She blinked and then gave him the most beautiful smile he had ever seen. "So that's what you look like under that mask."

He could not believe that is what she was thinking about after such an experience. "Should I put it back on?"

"For the love of god, don't you dare," Raven said as she looked at him. He was so

86

handsome. She stroked the side of his face and ran her thumb across his lower lip. "You are so handsome. I can't believe you hide this from the world."

Kioshi laughed softly and rested his forehead to hers. "You didn't answer my question. Are you okay?"

"I am over the moon," she said with a smile. "My word for someone who hasn't done that before you did it masterfully. All those books must have prepared you."

He groaned, "You have no idea how embarrassing that was when you were looking at those illustrations. I felt like a boy peeping into the girl's bathhouse."

Raven giggled, "I'm glad you had those books."

He could not remember a time he felt more relaxed than he did at that moment. Sex was incredible. It was a pleasure that surpassed any other pleasure. He looked down at her, smiling as he noticed how green her eyes were. He was surprised when he felt himself begin to harden again. Her eyes widened a bit, feeling it growing inside of her as well.

He chuckled, "I have a lot of years to catch up on. We might not leave this bed for quite a while."

Raven had no complaints as he began drugging her with those kisses of his once more and moving against her, slower and more sensual this time.

Chapter Seven

Kioshi lay staring at the ceiling in his room, the smell of lavender rolling in from the partially cracked window. He would have to close it soon as the temperature was already starting to drop outside. He was silently lamenting now having requested a long mission away from the village.

He was completely satisfied in a way that he did not know was possible. Raven was breathing softly next to him, completely wiped out from the hours of lovemaking. He had taken her in so many of the positions he had read about that there was not an area of her body that he did not know intimately now.

He could have gone another ten times, but he was sure she was going to be sore already from the countless times they had done into the twilight of night. He had been insatiable initially. It had to be the years of denial. Or perhaps it was her.

The more he made love to her, the more he felt connected and tied to her. It scared the hell out of him, but he had made his choice the minute he punched his friend. He grinned, now realizing exactly what Yoshiaki had been doing. He had been so filled with jealousy that he had been blinded to it, but his friend had intentionally tried to provoke him into doing what he really wanted, rather than what his brain was telling him to do.

Kioshi would have to apologize to him before leaving on the mission. He had not pulled that punch at all. He grinned in the darkness, knowing he would make it up to him one day. Raven gave a tiny shiver and he sighed. He sat up and closed the window, then lay back down next to her to draw her close. She nestled against him, wrapping an arm across his stomach.

He pulled the blanket up around them and breathed in her scent. He kissed the top of her head and stroked her arm. She smiled in her sleep.

"I love you, Kioshi," she said softly in her sleep.

He was surprised at the words and since she was asleep, he knew they had to be true. He held her closer and closed his eyes tight. The images of those that he had cared for in the past crossed his mind and his heart hurt. If something happened to her because of him, it would be his undoing. That had been his fear and he knew that his heart was already attached to her.

"I love you, too," he whispered.

Raven sat silently, watching Kioshi as he was packing for his mission. He had woken her up about thirty minutes before to let her know. She knew he would be given assignments but what rotten luck to have one the day after he finally claimed her as his own. And boy did he claim her.

She was sore from the number of times and different positions he had put her through. She never would have expected him to be that passionate with that kind of longevity. She hated that he was having to leave. Her only consolation was that he appeared to be just as upset about it.

She was enjoying watching him without his mask on. She gave a sigh as she looked at him. His eyes shifted over to her, his cheeks turned a little pink, and he laughed. "Are you really that into my face?"

"You have no idea," she said with a shy smile. "You are just... oh my god..."

She fell over in her giddiness while giggling. He laughed and walked over to her, pulling her up to kiss her before going back to packing the last of his supplies.

"That should just about be everything I'll need," he said with a heavy sigh. "I'm not sure when I will be back, but it will be at least a few months."

"I understand," she responded. "I'm going to miss you like crazy, just so you know."

Kioshi looked over at her and smiled, "I'll miss you too. I promise, I will be thinking about you a lot."

Raven felt her face warm at the sensual look he cast her. She came to her feet, wincing just a little as a few muscles protested. He grinned then came over to her. He held her tightly against his chest. "I want you to move out here. When I come home, I want to find you here."

Raven looked up at him in surprise, "Kioshi..."

"There is a lot I want to talk to you about but there is no time right now," he smiled and put his hand on the back of his neck. "I have to see Yoshiaki before I leave and apologize."

She gave a sigh of relief, "I'm glad you will. Honestly, Kioshi, we're just friends. We figured that out the first time we went out."

He gave a heavy sigh of relief at the words. He didn't realize that a part of him had worried that she had started to get feelings for his friend. He clasped her hand and pulled her across the room. He pushed a hidden panel and pulled out a packet with money in it.

"If something comes up while I am gone and you need extra money, this is here."

Raven felt her eyes burn, "Kioshi, I really don't-"

"Don't be stubborn. Just smile, say thank you, and relieve my mind that you'll be okay while I'm gone."

She laughed at his wearied tone of voice, "Thank you."

Kioshi grabbed her in a tight hug, lifting her feet off the ground. He breathed in deeply, memorizing her scent. He gave her one more kiss before lowering her to the ground.

"I'll be back as soon as this mission is complete," he promised.

Raven walked with Kioshi down the road to the central part of the village. His home was just on the edge of the village, backed up to the trees. She wondered just how much of the commotion his neighbors had witnessed. She felt her cheeks warm as they walked past a couple of them. Kioshi chose that moment to put his arm across her shoulders. She instinctively wrapped her arm around his lower back in a side hug. They smiled big at her from the action.

As they walked through the town, the expressions on everyone's face ranged from approval to shock. He was smiling the whole time and her face had to be at least ten shades of red. She felt like they were on parade.

"I wonder why everyone is so surprised," he said in that bored tone that he had perfected.

Raven covered her face and laughed. This would cause an uproar for days, weeks, possibly even months. The most confirmed bachelor was walking through town with a girl on his arm. Not just any girl, the one whom he had made quite a scene within the middle of the park the day before. The same girl that he had made another scene within the middle of the street a few days before that. His eyes were crinkled the whole time, showing that he was smiling big under his mask. As she gazed up at him, he was almost shining. She fell even more in love with him.

Yoshiaki was at the main gate out of town. He had a smug smile on his face. Raven winced as she saw that one side of his face was swollen and bruised. He did not look like he was angry with Kioshi though.

Kioshi extended his hand to him, reluctantly relinquishing his hold on Raven. "Thank you. I'm sorry for taking out my frustration on you."

Yoshiaki laughed, "It went all according to my plan."

Kioshi looked to Raven, "Keep an eye on her for me."

"Of course," he responded with a grin. "I would any ways. She is my friend."

He turned and looked at her one more time. She did not care that there were many eyes on them. She jumped up and gave him a tight hug. He laughed and spun her around.

"I'll return as soon as possible. Knowing you are waiting will make me take care of this faster."

Kioshi set her back on her feet and reluctantly went out the gate, meeting the other three members that would make up the team. She stood silently watching him leave until he disappeared from sight.

Naozumi stared at his advisor, Shinjiro, with a surprised expression. "Kioshi Sensei did what? With who?"

"He punched Yoshiaki at the park, then kidnapped the woman Yoshiaki had been with. It appears to have been a jealous rage because today he was seen with the same woman and was walking with her in a manner that conveyed, they are together."

Naozumi covered his mouth with his hand, trying hard to not laugh. "And the woman?"

"It's that lady from the other dimension, Raven."

Naozumi did laugh then, "I knew something like this would happen. I should have known he was close to losing it when he asked for an extended mission."

"What a pain, you know how much of an uproar this is going to have in the village? We're talking about a former leader of the village and one of our most famous shinobi."

Naozumi put a hand on the back of his neck and gave a nervous laugh, "And he is gone for an undetermined period of time. Well, I never thought it would be a quiet affair if Kioshi Sensei ever fell in love."

"He's too old for acting like this," Shinjiro said with a groan. "I mean, he's in his forties. He should be acting more dignified than this."

Naozumi laughed, "Like you acted with your wife?"

His advisor had the grace to blush at the reminder. "Point taken. So, what are we going to do about this?"

"Nothing. What is done is done. The village has seen bigger scandals than this. It will blow over on its own. Besides, I have a feeling we will be having a wedding as soon as he gets back to town. That is when things will blow up."

"What a pain," Shinjiro groaned.

Raven packed up the few items that she had to her name in a bag she had bought. She looked around carefully, making sure she had not forgotten anything. It seemed wild moving into Kioshi's home so soon after arriving but here she was getting ready to go. Butter was already at the

house. Yoshiaki had promised to take her there
while she packed up her things.

The final thing she did was write a thank
you letter to Naozumi, folded it up and put it and
the key inside an envelope. She left the little
apartment for the final time with a smile. If
someone had told her that she was going to be
this happy, she would never have believed them.

Before walking to her new home, she
went the opposite direction to the central
headquarters where Naozumi's office was located
at. She could still feel a blush on her cheeks as
people were pointing at her while whispering.
Several gave her smiles and nods of their heads.
This was probably going to go on for a while.

As she walked up to the main building,
the strangest feeling fell over her. She could not
place what it was, but it felt almost like power had
momentarily flared within her then disappeared.

She pulled open the large door and
walked inside the building. The secretary at the
front desk looked up at her as she approached.
A knowing look crossed her features, but she
maintained a professional demeanor.

"Raven, right?"

"Yes," she responded surprised. "This is
for Naozumi. Could you please pass it on to
him?"

"You could give it to him yourself... if
you wanted."

Raven was surprised by the words but all
she could think was "the audacity." She shook
her head negative, "No, I would not want to

bother him. He's a busy man. Thank you for passing it on to him."

She gave a nod of her head and Raven quickly retreated. She was beginning to feel strangely out of place and mind. She was ready to go hide at Kioshi's place. It took her about ten minutes to walk out to the house. She pulled the key he had given her out of her pocket and went into the house.

Butter romped up to her. Raven laughed, she looked like she was already settled. She had to smile, Yoshiaki had made a wooden dog bed for her and placed a blanket inside before leaving.

Raven shut and locked the door behind her. She had not forgotten the rogue ninja from the other night. While she was still in the village, she was also close to the woods and that made her a little nervous now that she was alone.

She walked into the bedroom and started unpacking the few things she had brought. The cleaning supplies she had left with the apartment for the next tenant. She opened his closet and smiled at the neatly hung rows of clothes. She leaned forward to smell them and gave a heavy sigh.

"This is going to be long couple of months," she sighed. "I already miss him."

Raven pushed his clothes over a bit and then hung her own next to them. She grinned as she looked at them hanging side by side. She liked the way that looked. It only took her a few minutes to unpack as she really had nothing to her name.

She sat down on the side of the bed and looked at her cellphone. It was almost dead now. She took a deep breath and looked at the plug next to the bed. "Here goes," she whispered. She cringed as she plugged it in, waiting to see if sparks erupted or her phone blew up from the wrong frequency of energy.

Neither happened. She gave a squeal of delight when the charging icon came across the screen. The image of her late husband was still on the lock screen. She took a deep breath, opened the phone, and then went to the photographs. She chose a picture of Kioshi she had saved from her world and put it on the lock screen instead.

When he returned, she would get photographs with him and of him first thing. Until then, she would have the images she had saved on her phone. She scrolled through her photographs and moved all the photos of her husband to a new folder that she had labeled Riley RIP.

She then went to the folder where all the photographs of her daughter were located. She smiled as she looked through them, once more remembering how wonderful it had been to be a mother, even if for a short period of time. Her eyes burned as she looked at her child.

As old as she was now, she doubted that there would be any more children. She felt bad because Kioshi deserved to be a father, but she remembered how long it had taken just to get her daughter and they had tried to have more immediately after her birth. She was the only child they had received in the ten years of their marriage. Raven believe that the problem lay with her.

She felt a small measure of guilt but shoved it away. She had to be thankful for what she did have and that was the man that she had loved for so long. It would be enough.

Raven opened her downloaded music and chose her collection of music that had a folk sound to it with artists like Passenger in the lineup. She smiled as the sound filled the house and she began looking around the home. It was not a large home by any estimation which was why the music could be heard throughout the residence.

She peered into his cabinets and was surprised to find a good supply of food inside. A lot of his was canned, pasta, or rice. Items that would last a long time. She supposed it was necessary since he would be gone on missions so often. Yet he had a large supply of spices and it did not take her very long to realize that he enjoyed cooking. He had items she never would have had in her own place just because she was rather basic when it came to cooking.

She looked in every nook and cranny. Some of the things she found did not make any sense to her. Other things had her in hysterics laughing. She turned several shades of red as she found his extensive book collection. To think he strolled around reading those without shame. She could not complain too much, they had been great inspiration for him.

Raven was most keen to find a box with photographs inside of it. She knew without having to read the back that they were of his father and mother. He had very few of his mother, but she was gorgeous. There was no doubting that he favored his father; however, little things like his lips and the cute birthmark just below them had come from her. Even the color of his eyes was his mothers.

She wondered why he kept them in a box instead of taking the best ones and framing them. Perhaps it was too painful for him. He had never really known his mother and his father had killed himself. She carefully set them back in the box and returned it from where she found it.

In another drawer, she found several medals and awards alongside the mask that he had worn when he was part of the Shadow squad. She felt like she had a deeper understanding of him by the time she had gone through the entire home.

She yawned as she took Butter out one final time. It was nice just opening the door and letting her run out to do her business. That would make getting ready for work easier and she would not have to get up as early. She was getting tired already. It had been an emotionally draining day.

When Butter came back to the door, she gave her a piece of carrot then went to the bedroom. She changed the music to new age and classical before curling up in the bed. She could still smell Kioshi's scent on the sheets. She smiled before falling into a deep sleep.

Raven was on her hands and knees scrubbing the floors of the kitchen for the short period that the cook was out of the area. The big pots were all in the front at that moment being kept warm for the customers that were coming in and out during the off hours.

It had been five weeks since Kioshi had left and she was finally not getting nearly as many looks. It probably helped that she did not spend a whole lot of time out and about. The only time she did go out was when Yoshiaki or Aoi made her. She had tried hooking him up with Aoi, but they did not make a match. She had been so disappointed when they didn't even give each other a glance.

Aoi was a sweetheart and had come to be her friend as they worked alongside each other. So now she had two friends she was playing matchmaker with. She would ask Aoi for suggestions for Yoshiaki and Yoshiaki for suggestions for Aoi. It was almost humorous going between the two.

So far, all the suggestions had not panned out. She was beginning to think it was a hopeless situation.

Raven had just finished cleaning the floors and dumping the dirty water out back when her stomach lurched. She groaned after emptying the contents of her stomach which was not much because it had been bothering her all day.

"Are you okay, Raven?"

She gave her a wobbly smile, "Yeah, just give me a minute. My stomach has been bothering me all day."

Aoi came up to her and pressed her wrist against her forehead. She frowned at her, "You feel cold and clammy. Maybe you should go home. You've finished most of your duties today. I'll tell father I sent you home."

Raven gave her a grateful smile and hung her apron up on the peg by the door. She slowly walked home, feeling a little better but still not entirely right. She let Butter out when she got home and was thankful the little dog did not take long. She skipped dinner and laid down on the bed.

She was so tired. Thankfully tomorrow was her day off so she could sleep in. She did not even bother turning on her music as she was almost instantly out the minute her head hit the pillow.

Raven slapped the hand that was bothering her. She tried to focus on whoever would not leave her alone, but her eyes would not focus.

"How long has she been like this?" A female voice asked.

"I don't know for sure. I checked on her when Aoi asked me to today since she had been sick yesterday." Yoshiaki's voice came to her. "It was late afternoon when I stopped in and she had not even taken her dog out yet. I'd say at least since she went home last night."

She could hear the woman gasp a little then laughed. "Oh my... Sensei..."

"What is wrong with her? Can you tell?"

"I won't be certain until we get her to the hospital. She is dehydrated from vomiting so much. Can you carry her?"

"Of course, Sora," he responded. "Hold on, Raven, we're getting some help."

Raven drifted back into the darkness as she felt herself being lifted.

Raven jerked as she finally came out of her deep sleep. She flinched as she saw a young woman leaning over her. She was smiling rather big at her and it took her mind a moment to realize who she was looking at. The bright colored, blue hair was her first indication. The green glow coming from her hand that was on her forehead was the second.

"Welcome back," Sora Neijing said with a bright smile. "You had Yoshiaki in a near panic."

"What happened?" She croaked; her throat was very dry. "Did I get the flu or something?"

Sora chuckled and helped her sit up. She then handed her a glass of water. "Drink that first. We've had you hooked up to IVs because you were dangerously dehydrated but I'm sure you'll feel better when you drink some water."

Raven took the drink, seeing the IV in her hand before she slowly drank the liquid. It felt good on her sore throat. She felt so weak it was pathetic.

"What happened? I remember going to bed but not much else after that."

"You apparently vomited most of the night. You must have been doing it unconsciously to not remember it."

Raven groaned, "No wonder my throat feels like it was dragged across gravel and glass."

Sora's eyes were dancing as she looked at her and Raven could tell that she could barely contain herself. She would have laughed at the expression if she hadn't felt like someone had kicked her ass.

"I have some news for you. I hope that it will not shock you too much. You're pregnant."

Raven felt her mouth drop open, "What did you say?"

"You're going to be a mother," she said with a grin. "I thought I sensed the life inside you when I was checking you out, but I was not sure until we examined you here. You're about five weeks along."

Raven felt her eyes burn and she put her hands over her stomach. "Seriously? I thought... I thought I couldn't..." She threw her arms around the younger woman. "Oh my god, this is a miracle!"

Sora laughed and hugged her back, "Oh, Kioshi Sensei will be so surprised when he gets back. I wish I was there when he gets the news."

Raven was so excited but also shocked. She bit her lower lip as she wondered how Kioshi would take the news. They had only just become lovers and the one night they were together they get pregnant?

"I still can't believe it," she whispered, folding her hands over her lower abdomen. "My late husband and I tried for years... I was certain I couldn't have children."

Sora gave her a look before hesitantly saying, "We gave you a complete check. There is absolutely nothing wrong with your reproductive system. It might have been your late husband, not you at all."

All the guilt she had been harboring for years lifted at the words and she felt tears rolling over her cheeks. To think, she was carrying Kioshi's baby. He would finally be a father and she would have the chance to be a mother again.

"I'll protect this little one with every ounce of strength I have in me," she whispered.

"We have some medicine that should help you to not be so sick. We've been giving it to you, and it appears to be working. You haven't vomited since we started giving it to you." Sora tilted her head to the side, "Yoshiaki said you had another child that died. Were you this sick with that child?"

"Oh no, not at all," she responded with wide eyes. "I actually had very little morning sickness. There were no complications, it was a good pregnancy."

"Hmm..." Sora shook her head, "Perhaps it is because you're.... um... an older expecting mother?"

Raven felt her face warm. Did she just call her old? Now she knew how Kioshi felt. "It's possible," she allowed.

"We'll run a few more tests before we release you just to cover any contingency. Your body isn't fully recuperated for you to go home yet regardless. So just rest for now. I'll check in with you later."

Several hours later Sora was looking at the results in front of her and she was mystified. She looked at her mentor and the top medical professional in the village for clarification. The older woman gave a heavy sigh.

"I can only assume it has to do with her unique physiology. I need to talk to her personally about this situation. She had to know what will happen."

Sora felt awful as she followed behind her mentor into Raven's room. She was staring out the window when they came in, dark circles were still under her eyes. Sora wished Kioshi Sensei was around, she needed him now.

Raven looked over at them and she could see that the other woman knew something was wrong. "Lady Takara, what is wrong?"

Sora was surprised that she knew her mentor's name. She probably should not have been, but she was all the same. Lady Takara grabbed a chair and pulled it up next to the bed. She sat down and folded her hands in front of her.

"All of your bloodwork and biological networks are in perfect condition. You're very healthy."

"But?"

"It must be because your physiology is so different from ours in terms of the chakra network. You have chakra but it flows very differently than ours and it is considerably weaker than our chakra." She leaned forward slightly, "During our pregnancies, the developing baby not only receives biological strength from the mother but also takes a considerable amount of chakra from the mother as well."

Raven frowned slightly, "What does this mean? I'm sorry, I'm a little confused."

"It is my opinion that this child's physiology is like ours, not like yours. We won't know for sure until you are much further along, and we can actually see the child." She took a big breath, "I believe, however, that is why you have become as sick as you have been. Your chakra is considerably weaker than ours and as the child grows, the more of your chakra it will take from you."

Raven pulled her legs up to her chest and wrapped her arms around them. Sora could see that she was starting to understand where Lady Takara was heading.

"This child may take so much of your chakra that you could potentially die in the process. You'll get weaker and weaker as time goes on and the child grows."

Raven straightened up on the bed, "I understand and I'm willing to take that chance."

Lady Takara gave a heavy sigh, "Then we will do everything in our power to help you get through this pregnancy. I'll start looking for ways to build up your chakra. There are some medications we can give you for now to help. You should be fine for the next few months. I would recommend you take it easy, no work, limited physical exertion."

Raven gave a sharp nod. "I'll do whatever I must to protect this child. This child must be born. My life doesn't matter but this child... Kioshi's line must continue. I know this sounds strange, but I believe it is very important to the future that this child lives."

Chapter Eight

Yoshiaki was going to make Raven crazy. He had literally built a house right next to Kioshi's to keep an eye on her. He had turned down all assignments that would take him out of the village and had adjusted his schedule to the hours when she was usually sleeping. She could barely go to the bathroom without hearing him ask if she was okay. You would think it was his baby the way he was behaving.

She was beyond exhausted as she lay on the elaborate wooden recliner that Yoshiaki had made just for her to relax outside. She absently rubbed her rounded belly. Six months along and no word from Kioshi. She was beginning to wonder if the baby would be born before he returned home.

Raven laughed imagining the look on his face if he came home that late. Welcome home, by the way... She barely recognized herself when she looked in the mirror. She was glad in an odd sort of way that Kioshi was gone. He would have been a wreck. She perpetually had dark, black shadows under her eyes, and she had lost weight rather than gained.

Her condition had put the medical team on high alert when they discovered she was carrying not one but two babies. They apparently could not determine the sex of the babies, but it was most definitely twins.

Raven was consuming large quantities of food but almost all the nourishment was going to them, not her own body. For that reason, they were gaining weight and getting bigger while she was losing weight and getting weaker. Everything she had was pouring into them.

Lady Takara had found special plants that was doubling her chakra but with the unexpected blessing of a second child within her, it was still taking more than was healthy for her. She could feel herself getting weaker and weaker as time went by.

She closed her eyes and leaned her head back. She felt as if she would not survive the pregnancy. Her heart ached, knowing Kioshi would blame himself. However, this time he would have his children to give him comfort. She just had to hang in there long enough to bring them into the world.

Lady Takara was already talking about a possible early delivery if her strength gave out before the end of the nine months. She had to carry them at least another month and a half to give them a fighting chance of survival.

The medical corps could keep them alive at that point, but any sooner and their chances dropped significantly. She prayed not for the first time that she would hold on until that time.

"I don't like the way you look, Raven," Yoshiaki said as his shadow fell over her.

She gave a heavy sigh, "You're worse than a mother, Yoshiaki. I'm fine for the moment, just very tired."

"I have to go shopping for supplies. Do you need anything special while I am out?"

Raven smiled at him, "Do you think you could bring me some dumplings? Those sound really good right now."

He grinned, "Absolutely."

"Oh, what I would do for some lemonade."

"Lemonade?"

"It's a special drink made from lemon juice and sugar. I don't know if y'all even have lemons."

"We have lemons," he smiled. "I will see if the market is carrying any right now."

Raven opened her eyes and smiled at him. "I know I've said it before, but I want to say it again, thank you. You truly are my best friend, Yoshiaki. You've gone above and beyond."

He blushed and put his hand on the back of his neck. He preened a little at the praise before giving her a goofy smile, "Do you need help going inside before I leave?"

"Yes, that might be a good idea."

He helped her to her feet and allowed her to lean heavily against him as they walked towards the house. He got her inside and back to the bedroom. She laid down with a yawn and he covered her with a blanket.

"I'll be back as soon as possible," he promised.

Raven nodded and silently watched him leave. She reached to the nightstand and grabbed her phone. She swiped to the playlist she had created for the baby then set the phone down on her massive belly. She almost laughed as one of the babies almost kicked the phone right off as soon as the music started playing.

It might be the end of herself, but she knew these children would be special. Kioshi would be an amazing father. She silently wished that she would make it to watch him with them, but she was slowly losing hope of it. Her strength was fading fast. She smiled as she was slowly pulled into sleep. She was more than happy to give all of herself for their lives.

Kioshi wearily rubbed his eyes as he jumped from tree branch to tree branch with his team. He was covered in dirt and blood as they hastily maneuvered back towards home. They had to get over the border before they could rest and refresh themselves. It had taken forever but they had finally completed their mission.

A few hours later, they were able to set up camp. He went to the river to wash the blood and grime off. He was feeling his age. It had been a while since the last long mission he had undertaken. This mission had seemed even longer as he was wanting nothing more than to be home with Raven.

He had decided that the minute he got home; they were going to be married. Distance had made no difference in how he felt about her. He loved her. It had been fast, but he knew that he loved her with everything he had. He grinned slightly; he had certainly been distracted enough since he left. Even his comrades had mentioned his lack of reading.

After Raven, the books paled by comparison.

The mission had taken a lot longer than he had thought it would take. He had thought to knock it out fast; however, one complication after another had risen. He was glad it was over and that they could go home.

His mind drifted as he wondered what Raven was doing. He half expected to come home and barely recognize the place. Women had tendencies to change things, but he had to admit, they did have a way of making a place feel more welcoming.

Kioshi ignored the conversation of his comrades as they talked amongst themselves. He stretched out on his bedroll, folding his hands behind his neck. The stars were bright that night and a gentle breeze was sliding through the trees. He closed his eyes and centered his breathing, allowing to pull and move through his body.

Something was wrong.

Kioshi opened his eyes and listened to the wind around him. Yet it did not feel like it was something near them. After stretching out his senses, he did not feel as if there was any danger to their party. Yet he could not shake the feeling that something was really wrong.

Yoshiaki quickly raced through the village, carrying Raven in his arms. They had been playing a game of cards when her eyes suddenly rolled up into her head and she fell over. He had managed to catch her before she slid to the ground. He had been growing more and more concerned. She had grown very thin, while her belly had grown very large.

She slept a good portion of the days and nights. He felt as if he had been watching her slowly die and it made him sick. Her skin tone was very pale, and her eyes had a continual shadow around them. She looked like death itself. Despite that, every checkup in town had revealed that the babies were not only growing strong but indeed were thriving.

"Damn it, Raven, don't you do this," he said to her, ignoring the looks of those that he passed on his way.

Words were not needed as he came into the hospital. Everyone had been on alert for this day since they discovered the unusual position of the pregnancy. The medical corps took her from him, and he watched helplessly as they wheeled her way.

Sora quickly ran to where Raven had been taken. She had sent word to Naozumi that what they all feared was happening. They had all been following the progressive decline closely, visiting her often in their free time. At first it had been for Kioshi's sake but over time, they had all come to really care for the woman of their beloved Sensei.

As she came into the room where she was at, everyone was already in high gear. She quickly washed her hands and put on scrubs. Raven had managed to fight for eight months, having passed the minimal mark a few weeks back.

As Sora placed her hands on her, she gasped as she sensed how low her chakra had fallen. There was hardly any left in her, and she could feel what little she had was being drawn into the twins within her body.

"We have to get them out now!" She leaned close to Raven, "Don't you give up now. Fight for your babies!"

Kioshi and his comrades all jumped into battle stances as a flash of what looked like fire suddenly slammed into the middle of their camp. He slowly lowered his kunai as he saw that it was Naozumi in full chakra mode. It had been a long time since he had seen his student use that form. Something was terribly wrong for him to arrive in that state.

"Kioshi, you have to come with me now," Naozumi commanded. "There is no time for explanation."

Kioshi put his kunai away, his heart dropping into his stomach. It had to be Raven. Naozumi securely took hold of him before abruptly streaking into the air. He had experienced the intense speed only one time before when the world was almost destroyed in the last Great War.

They crossed the vast distance in a matter of minutes. Before he knew it, they were landing in front of the hospital. Naozumi looked at him with his blue eyes, obvious distress in them. "It's Raven. She's dying."

Kioshi almost fell over at the words. He managed to force his legs forward as he pushed past his student and into the hospital. Yoshiaki pointed in the direction he assumed she had been taken and Kioshi sprinted down the hallway, despite the protests from the medical corps.

It took him only a moment to find the surgical room where she was at but was restrained from going in by Naozumi who had caught up with him.

"Kioshi, stop. You can't go in there."

It took every bit of his self-control to not throw his former student off and storm into the room. He could see Raven's face and she looked like she was already dead. She was very pale, and her eyes were darkly shadowed.

"What happened?" he asked in disbelief.

As if answering the question, he heard a sound that took his strength from him. A baby screaming. He leaned heavily against the window frame, watching as one of the nurses took the baby and brought it to a small table to clean it off. It was so small but its angry howl sounded strong.

He did lose the strength in his legs as a second baby joined the first. Naozumi lent him his strength, giving a little laugh.
"Congratulations, Kioshi Sensei, you're a father."

"How... What... When..."

"I don't think I need to tell you how or when it happened," Naozumi chuckled.

Kioshi shook his head and turned to look at his student, "I'm a father...." He then straightened to look in back at Raven, "What is wrong with her, why is she..."

Naozumi's expression changed, growing serious. "Her chakra network is vastly different than ours. It is not as strong. The babies as they have grown have taken more and more of her chakra than she has to give. We've been doing our best to keep her level up but the bigger they got, the weaker she got."

"I need to be with her," he whispered.

Naozumi gave a long sigh. He knew it was a waste of time trying to keep him from Raven any longer. He released his restraining hold on him and watched as Kioshi stormed into the operating room. Sora yelled at him, but he ignored her as he went to Raven's side.

Kioshi thought he was going to die as the medics worked hard to save Raven's life. He was calling himself every kind of fool. Sora had finally given up trying to make him leave. He had not even looked at her as he held Raven's cold hand tightly between his own. He would have willed his own chakra into her in that moment if it was possible.

He could hear the babies crying but right now, he could not look away from her. He leaned close to her ear, speaking softly, "Raven, I'm sorry. I should have been here. Had I known... I would have asked to be replaced. Please, fight. Don't give up now, I need you. Our babies need you. Don't make me do this on my own. Please, fight."

Kioshi was beginning to understand how his father must have felt when his mother had died giving birth to him. The thought of raising children alone was overwhelming. Even more so when he thought of how brief a time they had actually had together.

Harbinger of death. He was a harbinger of death. Everyone he loved died. He wanted to scream but all he could do was hold her hand tightly.

"Don't cry..." he suddenly heard her soft voice come to him. Kioshi raised his head to look at her. Her eyes were barely open, but she was looking at him, a weak smile on her face. "I can't take seeing you cry."

"Raven... don't you ever scare me like this again."

She laughed then promptly slumped. He straightened in horror, but Sora's voice calmed his heart. "It's okay. She just fell asleep. She's going to be okay. We got them out just in time."

Kioshi was in a state of shock as he sat in a lounge chair in Raven's room. In one arm he held his son. In the other arm he held his daughter. They were so small that he was scared if he moved, he would accidentally hurt one. They both seemed to be content sleeping in his arms.

Both babies had wisps of very thin, silver hair. The sight of it was doing strange things to his heart. He had never thought he would be a father and here he was to not one but two babies. He was overwhelmed by the emotions going through him.

"I knew you'd be a good father," Raven's voice came to him from the bed.

He looked up and met her eyes across the room. She looked exhausted but she was smiling. "I'm sorry. I should have been here, Raven."

She smiled, "You had no idea and you were not in a place where we could even tell you. Why are you beating yourself up about it?"

"You almost died."

She chuckled, "But I didn't."

Kioshi stared at her for a long moment. "I love you, Raven. I should have told you before I left."

Raven gasped at his words, his dark eyes looking at her as intently as he had the day he had claimed her. She felt tears go over her cheeks. He loved her? She wiped at her eyes.

"I never thought you'd say that to me."

His eyes crinkled as he smiled, "I will make sure to say it many times in the years to come."

"I love you so much too," she finally said. "I have loved you for a long time now."

She watched as he carefully came to his feet and walked over with their babies. She was in awe and he transferred one, then the other into her arms. He sat on the side of the bed, watching her as she looked at them.

"Oh my gosh... they are so precious, and they have your hair!" She gushed, "That is absolutely adorable. Are they..."

"This is our son and this one is our daughter."

118

"Oh Kioshi... one of each," she smiled.

He shifted a little, worried at how she would feel about the next. "I made a decision for you, Raven. You may be very angry with me, but I felt it was for the best."

She looked up at him.

"While you were still open, I told them to make it to where you can't have any more children."

Raven felt a moment of anger before she let out her breath in a rush. She looked at the two children in her arms. She survived this pregnancy but the next one might very well kill her. She did not like that she was not part of the decision but the more she thought about it, the more she realized she would have chosen the same eventually.

"It's okay," she finally spoke. "We have these two, it is enough."

He let out a pent-up breath, "I am glad you agree. I was actually worried you'd try to punch me again."

She laughed, "If I recall that didn't work too well the last time. Besides... I have my hands full right now."

Kioshi's eyes crinkled with his silent laughter. He pulled his mask down and leaned forward to kiss her. She melted all over again.

"I can't believe it. It took all these years to finally see what your face looked like!" Naozumi exclaimed from the door.

Kioshi groaned before looking over at him. Behind Naozumi was Sora and her husband Shiro. All three of them were gaping at his uncovered face. He looked back at Raven and his facial expression was priceless. He had spent years keeping them in suspense as to what he looked like and in one moment, they finally got to see because he had wanted to kiss her.

"Now see what you did?" He said in that tone of his.

Raven laughed loudly, waking the babies in the process. She could not stop laughing even as she tried to soothe the babies back to sleep.

"Not bucktoothed," Shiro commented.

"Nor big lipped," Sora agreed.

Naozumi laughed with Raven, remembering when they had theorized what Kioshi Sensei was hiding under that mask. It had made them crazy for years, but eventually they had given up ever seeing as he had outmaneuvered them time and time again.

Kioshi pulled his mask back up and rolled his eyes. He rubbed the tops of each baby's head; the hair was incredibly soft. "I would have thought the mystery would be a bore to you all by now, especially after everything that has happened."

"I have to admit, I'm a little disappointed," Naozumi responded. "You're actually normal under there."

Raven laughed, "Mmm, a little better than normal."

"You are biased," Kioshi responded in a bored tone.

"Can we... hold them?" Naozumi finally asked after a moment of silence.

Kioshi stared at his son for a long time. His little face was relaxed in sleep. His daughter was in the small bed next to Raven, sleeping alongside her mother for the time being. His son had woken briefly and wanting to give Raven some rest, he had picked him up and taken him to the rocking lounger by the window. He had fallen back asleep rather quickly, his little hand curled around his index finger.

The feelings he had looking at his son were indescribable with words. His eyes were almond shaped like his own, making him believe as he got older, he would look like him. They had yet to name either child.

"I certainly was not expecting you or your sister," he said softly. "I am glad you are here, but I will admit, I don't know how good of a father I will be. I have made a lot of mistakes in my life, but I will do my best to not make them with you both."

He rubbed the little guys head with his thumb. The hair was so soft, and he felt overwhelming love come on him. He was a gift. He pulled his mask down before leaning forward to kiss the top of his little head.

"I will teach you all that I know, which will be a lot. You will be the future of the village and I will ensure you will be a leader in your generation." He shifted his eyes to Raven, "I will teach you to protect those that you love with everything you have. Most importantly, I will teach you the value of teamwork."

The baby yawned and he almost laughed. He already had a bit of his father's attitude.

"I hope you get your mother's enthusiasm and compassion," he finally spoke. "Don't be as hard as I am. Be willing to open your heart, but only when they show you they are worth it."

Raven quietly opened her eyes to look at Kioshi. Never had she seen a man so engrossed in a baby. Even Riley had not been that intense. Kioshi was completely unaware of anything else in the room. His mask was down even though it was possible anyone could come into the room at any time. He was talking so softly she could barely hear what he was saying.

In all her days, she would never forget this moment.

Those dark eyes shifted to her. He smiled at her, having known all along she was awake. "Marry me, tomorrow. When we take them home, I want us to truly be a family."

"Yes," she responded. "I will marry you."

Chapter Nine

Time had passed quickly. Raven had almost completely forgotten her life in the other world. It seemed like such a far distant memory after everything that had happened since coming to this world. She was excited as she watched her son, Oshin, weaving on his feet as he tried to steady himself.

"Kioshi, he's going to do it," she said excitedly as the toddler took his first wobbly step forward. He looked so proud as he was chewing on the toy in his hand and toddling forward. He sank down to his butt. "Yes, Yes, Yes! Awesome, Oshin!"

He was adorable. He looked like a tiny version of Kioshi except his eyes were lighter. She suspected they might end up being the same color as her own or even possibly blue like her father's had been.

Kai on the other hand looked like a good mix between the two of them. She had her father's dark eyes, but her skin tone was that of her mother's. Her facial shape was also like her mom's, but her lips and nose were just like her father's. She even had the cute little birthmark just below her lips that her father had; not that many people would know that since he wore his mask all the time.

Both children had kept the silver hair that they had inherited from their father. It was adorable in Raven's opinion and would be quite striking as they got older.

"He's advanced," Kioshi responded in approval.

"I wonder who he got that from," Raven said with a laugh before scooping Kai up into her arms from where the little girl had been playing with Butter.

"Hmm, I do wonder."

Raven looked at Kai and shook her head. "Don't you worry, Kai. It might take us girls a little longer, but we always end up coming out on top."

Her daughter grinned at the words. She gave her mom a wet kiss that had Raven laughing.

Kioshi grabbed up Oshin and followed Raven into the bedroom. It was the twin's naptime. Kai was usually quick to settle down and go to sleep but Oshin... He was a stubborn little guy and not a fan of naps. It was for that reason Kioshi would start his nap in their bed before transferring him over to his bed. He was more agreeable when curled up with his father.

Raven nuzzled Kai's head, loving the smell of her baby girl. She kissed her before setting her down in the crib that Yoshiaki had made as a gift to them. Kai grabbed her favorite stuffed animal, shoved a thumb in her mouth, and rolled onto her side.

"Now Oshin, it's time to nap," Kioshi was trying to reason with the seven-month-old.

Oshin narrowed his eyes on his father in mutiny. Raven had to cover her mouth to hide the laugh. He was as stubborn as his Daddy. He shook his head no. Kioshi narrowed his own eyes back at the boy. It was a battle of wills and Oshin had no chance.

Raven slipped out of the room before she broke into laughter. It was the daily laugh that she got as father and son battled one another. Kioshi left the bedroom sooner than she expected. She was picking up toys when she felt his hands on her hips, pulling her back against his obvious desire.

She sucked in a breath and dropped the toys as she straightened up. His lips were almost instantly on her neck, one of his hands sliding down the front of her pants, the other sliding up the front of her shirt to knead one breast. Kioshi never wasted an opportunity.

Raven moaned as he found her clit with expertise. His lips on her neck were driving her crazy. "I want to hear you moan but if you get too loud, you'll wake the monsters."

She bit her lower lip at the soft reproach. He easily unlatched her pants and dropped them before nudging her a few steps to bend her over the table. She gasped as he thrust into her from behind. His hand slipped over her lips to stifle the moan he knew was coming.

After several thrusts, he abruptly pulled himself out and turned her around. She let out a started gasp as he set her up on the table before slipping back into her front the front. His mouth and tongue were making her forget everything but his taste. He would whisper wickedly delicious things between kisses, knowing they made her crazy.

It did not take long for her to climax. He smothered both of their cries by pressing their lips tightly together as he emptied himself inside of her. He was breathing hard in her ear before he reluctantly pulled out.

"I look forward to when we can make as much noise as we want," he chuckled against her neck. "I love your moans."

"That's probably going to be a while," she laughed, kissing his chin.

"Only three and half more years," he responded in that bored tone of his that made her love him even more. "Then they will be in the academy during the day and I can have you all to myself."

Raven laughed as she pulled her clothes back into place. He was an insatiable beast, but she loved it. "And you'll probably be busy with missions or on patrol."

"I will never be too busy for that," he responded with a devilish grin. "Still mad that I'm going to be gone a few days?"

"I'm not mad," she protested.

"Ah, okay, pouting."

She jabbed him in the gut with her finger and he made a display of injury, but his eyes were laughing.

"So long as you don't disappear for eight months, I can live with a couple of days," she finally said.

"Naozumi promised that those long missions were over unless something very drastic required my skills," Kioshi told her with a smile. "If he said it, it is as good as done. My role was bound to change even if you and the twins had not come along. I cannot stop the process of time."

Raven hugged him tight. "Now don't start that. You're not anywhere near being old. Mature, yes, but not old."

"A couple of kids called me grandfather the other day," he groused.

She laughed hard at the words and the expression on his face. "Oh Kioshi, it's only because kids think anyone that is over twenty is old. You have many years of sexiness ahead; I promise you that. You'll be one of those really old guys that still make the ladies drool."

Kioshi's face turned red at her words. He gave her a hard, melting kiss. He grinned, swatted her on the backside then went to the door. He grabbed his pack, swung it onto his back and gave her one last sensual look before pulling his mask up and going out the door.

Raven gave a long sigh and leaned against the table. That man was an addiction.

Concealed in the shadows, one of darkness and loathing watched as his nemesis left the village with a team. Hatred swirled in his heart, desiring to crush him into dust. Kioshi Hamasaki had ruined everything, and he would pay the price for that. He would take what he held most dear and bleed the life out slowly before his eyes. He would not kill him personally. He wanted him to suffer for many years, just as he had suffered. He had waited for what seemed an eternity to find a weakness but there had been none. Finally, after all these years, he had a weakness.

Pain will take on a new meaning for you, Kioshi. I swear it upon the blood of my ancestors. You will want to do what your father did once I am done.

"Trust me, this will be fun for us," Hikari said with a big smile on her face. "Benjiro will have lots of laughs with Oshin and Kai. Take a few hours for yourself. I know as a mom that it is hard to get some things done."

Raven smiled with thankfulness. She had come to really enjoy the soft spoken Hikari. "I appreciate this so much. I would never have thought to ask..."

"I understand," she responded with a bright smile. "Now go. Get out of here and enjoy your time."

Raven quickly kissed each twin before hurrying away. There was so much she wanted to do in the time that Hikari had unexpectedly given her. It had been a while since she was able to go about on her own. She felt almost like a giddy schoolgirl as she went about town.

"Long time no see," Aoi said as Raven sat down on the barstool and ordered a bowl of her favorite Ramen.

"It has been a while, hasn't it?" Raven responded with a laugh. "Hakari has given me the afternoon off."

Aoi laughed, "Oh that should be fun for her with all three of those babies playing."

Raven enjoyed chatting with her friend as she ate the ramen. She left feeling full and rejuvenated. As she walked down the street, she had an almost uncomfortable feeling fall over her. She slowed as she tried to identify what was wrong, suddenly feeling thankful she had taken the precaution of wearing her gun that day. Kioshi had admonished her to always be aware, especially when he was gone. He had even gone so far as to try to train her how to use a kunai. It had been a rather comical experience but eventually she had grown accustomed to it. She still preferred her gun, although she would have to find someone that could make replacement cartridges for her.

Kioshi had mentioned a weapons dealer that possibly could figure out how to copy the mechanics of her bullets. He had been putting off taking her there and since she now had some free time, she was going to get it done.

The streets were busier than usual. She looked around, trying to see if there was anyone that was out of the ordinary. She did not know everyone in the city, but she assumed someone up to no good would stand out. She was wrong. She did not see anyone or anything, but she could not shake the feeling that something was definitely wrong.

As she found the shop, she looked over her shoulder one last time before slipping inside. By the time she left, she was excited. The shop owner was confident he could reproduce the bullet by reverse engineering it. That was a relief to her because she was never going to be a shinobi and she wanted something that she could use if danger loomed and Kioshi was not there.

Raven gasped as several explosions rocked the village. Screams from the villagers made the streets one of chaos as everyone started running for safety. The ground beneath her feet shook from one of the closer explosions. Her first thought was her babies and she started running in the direction of Naozumi and Hikari's home.

As she passed an alley, someone lunged out and grabbed her, trying to drag her into the alley. Her scream was drowned out by the screams of so many others at the chaos that was happening from the multiple explosions. Raven had the presence of mind to grab the kunai on her belt and stab the man that had hold of her.

He cried out and dropped her in surprise. He had clearly not been expecting that from her. She quickly replaced the kunai and went for her gun as she put distance between the two of them. She kept her weapon on him, ignoring the chaos around her.

"Who are you?"

The man across from her was wearing a long black robe. His face was covered in white war paint with black markings that made him look like a skeleton. His pale hair was slicked back, and his eyes were a chilling shade of violet. He surprisingly did not look familiar to her.

He did not answer and instead pulled out a jagged sword so quickly she barely had time to see it. She immediately started firing at him. She was shocked as he appeared to deflect every shot, she fired at him. She was almost certain though that at least two of them had found their mark but he did not stop moving. She cried out as his blade knocked her gun from her hand and the sword sunk into her flesh.

Raven could taste blood in her mouth. He was obviously angry as he yanked the blade out, ripping her open even more, before grabbing her by her hair. He flipped her in front of him as a shield. Her abdomen and back, where the blade had exited on entry, were on fire and her legs were shaking from the wound. She was scared to even look down, thinking she would see her own guts hanging free.

She could see several members of the Shadow patrol had arrived, most likely drawn to the discharge of her weapon. It had its own unique sound after all. He had not planned for that either. She had a feeling that the explosions were diversionary. He had intended to discretely grab her in the chaos, but she had thrown a wrench into those plans.

She felt a second blade come up to her neck in warning. "Tsk, tsk. Step back or I'll slice her open. It won't be as satisfying as I want but I will do it."

His voice sent a chill down her spine. She got the immediate impression he was going to kill her regardless of what happened. It just all depended on how fast.

"Just take him," she told them as she spit out blood. "He's going to kill me either way."

"Silence, you stupid bitch," he growled in her ear.

Raven could see Yoshiaki edging closer while weaving hand signs. All the guards were wearing their traditional masks, but she knew exactly which one was him.

"Tell Kioshi, I will have what is his where the blood moon touches the horizon. Life for life, pain for pain." She cringed in repulsion when he licked the blood that had rolled out the side of her mouth. "The Tobirami will have their revenge."

Raven gasped as she felt them both suddenly being sucked into a portal and transported away. It was instantaneous. One moment she was in the village, the next they were in a creepy cave with several other men. He yanked her hard by the hair in obvious anger before shoving her hard into the wall.

She grunted at the impact, tasting more blood in her mouth. She felt as well as heard her nose crack on hitting the hard rock surface. She dropped to one knee and spit out the blood in her mouth once again. Her hands were shaking as she carefully touched the wound where she had been stabbed. She almost cried in thankfulness that she did not have any organs hanging out, but her hands were covered in blood rather quickly.

"Make sure she does not go anywhere," he barked at the others. "No medical treatment, I did not hit any vital points. I want her to feel every bit of the pain she is feeling right now. Prepare yourselves, our revenge is at hand!"

A cheer went up from the men as she sank down to her butt, clasping her hand over the wound. Perhaps it was the knowledge that she was going to die either way that gave her the courage to mouth off to him, but she could not help herself.

"Just fucking kill me now, you sick bastard."

A maniacal laugh left his lips before he came over to her, grabbing her by the throat and lifting her up in the air with one hand. She clawed at his hand as black spots started to appear before her eyes and tried to kick him.

"That would be too soon, way too soon," he crooned. "I want Kioshi to watch as I slowly take the life from you. I might even skin you alive just for the fun of it. I want him to lose his mind and regret the day that he dared to oppose the Tobirami."

She sucked in air hard as he abruptly dropped her and turned away. Her throat felt crushed and each gasp of air was painful as it slid through the airway.

"He's going to kill you," she managed to croak out. "You've done signed your own death warrant."

He laughed before coming back over to her. He shoved a few fingers into the wound she was clutching, causing her to scream in pain. The pain took her breath away. She really needed to keep her mouth shut. He then pulled them out and licked the blood from his fingers. It was so repulsive she almost vomited as she gasped for air.

"I'm going to let you in on a little secret, my dear," He began sending a chill down her spine. "I am unstoppable, almost invincible. Did you not wonder how your miraculous weapon did not leave even a single scratch on me? Oh, it made impact, several times in fact. I regenerate and heal on a level you cannot comprehend. Kioshi can come at me with all he has, and it will not be enough to stop me."

He grabbed her chin and turned her face to the right then the left. The expression he was giving her made her extremely uncomfortable.

"I expected the babies to be with you," he spoke finally, sending a chill down her spine. "Had they been anywhere but with Naozumi they would be here with you. Now they are out of my reach; however, know this... Once I dispense with you and break Kioshi, I will then destroy his seed. He will have no legacy left except suffering. This I decree."

"You'll never get my babies."

He laughed as he released her chin, "I see why he likes you. You just don't know when to stop do you?"

"What does it matter, you're going to kill me regardless? Death comes to us all. Do you really think I'd fear a pathetic piece of shit like you?"

Raven winced as he grabbed her once more and pulled her close to his face. "Oh no, you will not provoke me into killing you quickly. The more you anger me, the slower your death will be and the more I will enjoy it."

"Fuck you," she said before she spit into his face.

Blissful darkness followed as he slammed her head into the rock behind her with enough force to knock her out.

Naozumi was silent as Kioshi abruptly came into his office. The wrath that was on his face was undeniable, even with the mask. The air almost crackled with the energy he was building within himself from his fury.

"Before you play into his hands, Yoshiaki was able to plant a tracing seed on her before they teleported away. He's already on his way tracking them with a Shadow team. Once he has a location, he will send word back to us."

"Do you know who took her?"

"No," Naozumi responded. "No one, not even Yoshiaki recognized him. Do you know who the Tobirami are?"

Kioshi stilled before him. "They're gone. Before you were even born, we were ordered to eliminate them. They were a radical cult group that slaughtered people indiscriminately that refused to convert and worship their leader, a man named Uzaki."

"It could be this Uzaki that took her then," Naozumi pondered.

"No, I killed him with my own lightning blade," Kioshi said softly. "I assure you; he is dead."

"Then one of his followers," Naozumi responded. "I have your children under heavy guard. They are safe. We can be thankful that they were not with Raven when all of this happened."

Kioshi turned on his heel and started towards the door.

"Where are you going?"

"I'm going after Yoshiaki," Kioshi responded. "I'm not waiting for them to send word. When she is located, I will bring her home immediately."

"Kioshi Sensei, wait!"

Naozumi frowned as the door shut behind him. There was no stopping Kioshi.

Chapter Ten

The pain was intense. Raven wanted to scream it hurt so bad, but she refused to give her captors the satisfaction. It felt like the sword was still inside her body and sawing at every movement of her body. In addition to that, her head was throbbing. She had already thrown up once. She was having a hard time keeping her eyes open as her strength was bleeding out of her.

She had to figure out how to get loose before Kioshi walked into his trap. Or get the maniac, that she had heard one of the men refer to as Draidan, to kill her before he could torture her. The second option had not panned out very well. He was rather intent on killing her slowly in front of Kioshi. He did not seem to want to kill Kioshi. No, he wanted to break his spirit and she could not be the cause of that. She had complete faith Kioshi would find a way to stop him, even if he did have the healing ability he boasted of.

That left option one as the primary option.

Raven felt hopeless as she looked around the cave. The men were not watching her very closely. If she had some strength, she might have been able to slip away but after losing so much blood she was weakened considerably. It was probably for that reason that they were not watching her as closely as they should have been doing. She wasn't even restrained.

Draidan was nowhere to be seen. She had only seen him briefly after being roughly brought back to consciousness. That was at least an hour ago... at least it felt like an hour ago. She slowly tried to come to her feet as they became distracted by putting two animals in a caged area to fight.

The pain was breathtaking. It took every bit of her energy move even the little bit that she did. She closed her eyes for a moment and the image of her beloved came to mind. No, she had to push past it. Even if she could not escape the cave, if she could find a place to hide, Draidan could not use her against Kioshi.

Slow steps, her eyes on the men yelling at the fighting animals. She froze when she thought one of them saw her but then moved faster to the first passageway that was closest to her. She felt a small measure of relief as darkness enclosed around her as she pressed blindly forward. She hoped to god she was not leaving a trail of blood behind her.

Her eyes were starting to adjust to the darkness. The further she went, the more the pain climbed. She had to find some kind of hidey hole soon or she was going to pass out and be found easily.

It had probably only been a short period of time, but it felt like an eternity before she found a very thin opening in the wall. She had to suck in her gut, scraping the wall the entire way in. Claustrophobia clawed at her, but she forced herself to keep going. She had to get far enough in that if they looked, they would not see her. She was surprised when it abruptly opened into a small hollow. The path ended there, and she knew it was as far as she could go. She slid down the wall, tucking her legs to the side where they would not be seen if anyone looked down the narrow path she had taken.

She then allowed herself to cry silently from the pain and fear. At least now he could not use her against Kioshi. She wondered if she would bleed out in that little hollow in the cave. Her remains might never be found. So be it. In the distance, she could hear yelling and scrambling. She smirked in the dark and closed her eyes.

Her mind drifted for a long while between the past and present. She saw her daughter that had passed and smiled. She could clearly see her running through fields of beautiful white flowers. Somewhere she drifted between consciousness and eternity. She even saw Riley walking behind Leia, a beautiful smile on his face as he watched their daughter.

She jumped a little as something slithered across her hand, dragging her back to the present. She frowned but did not jerk her hand away. She never had a fear of snakes and it was better if she did not move just in case it was poisonous. It would go away eventually.

A loud commotion that seemed to be getting closer to her reached her hearing. She made herself as small as she could, hoping that she went unseen or unfelt. Her lower chakra would come in handy if they had a sensitive looking for her. She was sure with her injuries it was even lower.

Raven covered her mouth with her hand to stifle her breath as light appeared through the crack she had maneuvered through earlier. A rock moved and she cursed inwardly. She then almost cheered as the snake slithered past her to chase the light shining down the passageway.

"It's just a damn snake," the person at the end said.

"We should still go in and check to make sure she's not hiding in the back," another voice said.

"Do you see how small this is? There is no way she could have fit down there. We'll get stuck if we try."

"I am not going back to Draidan without looking," the other man responded with fear in his voice. "If she's in there and we don't look, we are dead."

"You do what you want, I'm not hanging around."

Raven closed her eyes tightly as she heard one set of footsteps recede. The unmistakable sound of someone squeezing down the narrow entrance reached her ears. She looked around the partly illuminated area she was squeezed into for anything she could use as a weapon.

A jagged rock lay not far from her in the tiny area. She wrapped her hand around it and waited as he came closer. As his head cleared the opening, she swung with all her strength. Blood splattered from the impact, but it was not enough to take him down. He gave a curse as he tried to

subdue her in the tiny space as she swung again
and again.

Her head rang as he backhanded her
hard. Little rocks were falling as she fought
against him. He knocked the rock out of her
hand and hit her full force in the temple. Her
head spun and she partially blacked out. When
she came to, he was dragging her out of the
crevice. She gave a shriek and started kicking
him while grabbing at the wall, looking for any
kind of hold.

"You bitch," he growled as he yanked
her the rest of the way out of the crevice.

At that same moment, the cave
shuddered and rocked from an explosion. Raven
laughed at the sound.

"You're so screwed," she wheezed.

He kicked her hard across the ribs, the
tip of his shoe hitting the open wound. She
screamed from the pain and almost blacked out
again. He then grabbed her by the legs once
more and started dragging her down the tunnel.

Kioshi caught up with Yoshiaki quickly.
It was not long before they were all perched
outside a cave in the mountain. All on his
journey he had been pooling his chakra. He
knew that his anger and fear was clouding his
judgment, but he could not find a way to bring it
under control.

"She's inside," Yoshiaki spoke softly.
"We should request backup. We have no idea
how many of them are in there."

"You go ahead and do that, I am going in," Kioshi responded softly.

He expected an argument and was surprised when Yoshiaki did not argue but instead looked to one of his men to say, "Send word to the village of our location. The rest of us are going ahead." He then turned his focus back to him. "Raven is my friend. I was going to go in the moment we found her, even before you found us. So... how are we doing this?"

"We are going to split up," Kioshi looked over at him. "I'm going to create a diversion. His focus is going to be on me. I want you and your team to find Raven. The primary objective is to get her out of there."

Yoshiaki gave a nod before motioning his team in another direction. Kioshi hesitated only a moment before leaping forward. He reached the cave shortly and immediately encountered resistance. He quickly weaved hand signs as he ran forward to meet them head-on. His right hand glowed with electricity as it became the lightning blade. In his left hand, he held a kunai. He went through the men as if they were nothing. They fell beneath the two weapons easily, no match for one of his strength and ability.

As he reached a barrier in the mouth of the cave, he reared his right arm back and slammed it into the barrier with the full force of his lightning blade. It exploded inward upon the contact.

As he stepped over the threshold, three men were sprawled having been killed by the explosion. His eyes narrowed into the darkened area beyond as he carefully walked inside the devil's lair.

Kioshi knew without being told which of the men was in charge. He could sense the huge amount of chakra the man held. He raised his hand with the kunai, meeting the man's violet eyes without hesitation.

"You requested my presence?" He asked, purposefully infusing boredom into the words. "I do not recognize you, but I suppose that does not matter since I will be killing you soon."

A maniacal laugh echoed off the walls as the man stepped forward without fear. Kioshi narrowed his eyes as he took in the skeleton pattern that had been painted on his face. Something vaguely familiar pinged at him from the far recesses of his mind. As he tried to mentally peal the makeup off, he realized that he could not have been very old at the time of their last encounter.

Kioshi himself had been a teenager when he had gone into that battle. As he looked at the violet colored eyes, he suddenly realized why the man had plotted for so long.

"You are Uzaki's son."

His mind flashed back in time. He could see his hand in the lightning blade pierced straight through Uzaki. As he looked to the left, hiding under the bed had been a small boy with eyes the color of violet. His face had been expressionless.

143

Kioshi had been ordered to eliminate everyone, but he had left the child untouched. He could not kill a child. Now as he stood before that same child that was now a man, he questioned that moment of mercy.

"There is a reason that entire villages are slaughtered, leaving no survivors. The greatest nations discovered when they did not lay waste to the most dangerous of people, that those that they had spared would rise up later." His nemesis spoke as if reading his mind. "Yes, you did make a foolish mistake thinking that I would just be grateful for sparing my life. You destroyed my future that day and I lived with the memory of you slaughtering my father."

Kioshi watched him warily, hoping that Yoshiaki had found Raven already since she was not with Uzaki's son.

"My mind was splintered for a very long time... then I realized something. I am more powerful than my father. As charismatic as he was, he lacked the power to dominate. I inherited the power of my mother's people. On that day, I knew that I had to show you what true suffering is... I have no intention of killing you today, Kioshi. That is too merciful. I will break your spirit and take you to the same place that your father was all those years ago."

A scuffle caught Kioshi's attention. The man in front of him smiled very wide. He watched as Raven was dragged into the chamber. She was shrieking and fighting like a wild animal. He almost laughed because the man that had hold of her looked like he had lost the upper hand a couple of times. *That's my girl.* At the moment, she was throwing random rocks at his head when her hands would find one.

He looked ready to kill her when he finally tossed her at his nemesis' feet. "Lord Draidan, I found her in a small alcove in one of the corridors."

"Excellent," he responded.

Kioshi almost smiled. She had escaped from them, at least temporarily. As he shifted a glance at her, he felt pride. She surprised him. She was so dirty from her fight that he could not assess at a glance her injuries. Her face was swollen on one side, her eye almost closed. He saw blood on her clothes, but he was not sure where it was coming from.

Raven felt like one giant wound and wanted to cry in frustration as she was dumped in front of Draidan. Her eyes moved to where Kioshi was standing. His gaze met her own briefly as he was keeping his attention firmly on his nemesis. Yet in that moment she felt peace settle on her. He had a plan; she could feel it.

"Kioshi, his ability is to heal very quickly!"

Raven screamed as Draidan slammed his sword down and through her right thigh. She felt it go straight through, cutting tendons yet somehow missing the main artery. She felt skewered and instinctively she tried to grab the sword and pull it out. In the process she sliced her hands.

"Too bad that isn't the case for you, my dear," Draidan spoke. "You really should learn when to shut up."

Kioshi moved so fast that Raven's eyes could hardly keep up with him. The sword was yanked out of her leg as Draidan barely deflected the attack that came at him. She cursed as blood suddenly spurted from the wound, the blade having nicked the artery on its way out. She clasped her leg, trying to stop the bleeding and failing unsuccessfully as blood ran like a river between her fingers.

The man that had found her suddenly grunted above her and she looked up. A piece of wood was protruding from his chest. His eyes rolled up into his head as blood spilled freely out of his mouth. He dropped to the ground behind her. Vines snaked out of nowhere and wrapped around her. She was suddenly yanked backwards, and in a moment, Yoshiaki was holding her in his arms.

The vines he had used to drag her abruptly back, to where he had discretely arrived, left her body then wrapped around her leg. She hissed as they tightened abruptly, creating a tourniquet. She cried from the pain and he held her closer.

"I'm sorry," he said softly. "I'm getting you out of here now while Kioshi is keeping him busy."

Raven turned her eyes to where Kioshi and Draidan were battling. She was mesmerized watching Kioshi. His movements were fast, precise, and greater than she could have ever imagined. Watching him as an anime was nothing compared to watching him in the flesh. The lightning blade, which was pure chakra in the form of electricity surrounding his hand, was slicing with deadly precision. Every time it contacted Draidan or his blade, it would knock him back a few feet.

Kioshi was raining hell fire down upon him, yet despite the severity of the blows the other man was healing so quickly they had little effect on him.

"Wait, Yoshiaki," she pleaded. "He's going to need your assistance to take him down. He heals so quickly that everything Kioshi is doing is not hurting him."

Yoshiaki turned his dark eyes to the battle and it only took a moment to see what she was saying. He motioned to one of his men, "You're still leaving."

"But-"

He raised a finger in warning and gave her a rather menacing look before turning his eyes to the Shadow fighter that was with him. "Get her to safety immediately."

The masked fighter gave a nod of his head before lifting Raven in his arms and racing away from the battle. Raven looked past his shoulder, straining to watch Kioshi for as long as she could.

"Hold tight," the man holding her said before increasing his speed ten-fold the moment they left the cave.

Her last image of Kioshi was of him in a high downward leap, lightning blade coming down with full force at Draidan's head. The other man was driven into the rock surface with enough force to split the ground around him.

Chapter Eleven

Kioshi was relieved as he saw Raven being hauled out of the cave from the corner of his eye. He was even more relieved as Yoshiaki joined his side in the battle. Raven had been more than correct when she gave her warning about his healing ability. It did not seem to matter how much he hit him with, he recovered so quickly that he barely got a breathier in to recoup the chakra he was expending. He had only seen this one other time and it had been Naozumi that had subdued the villain.

He almost groaned as Draidan started pushing himself back up out of the crater his last hit had folded around him. Wood abruptly erupted out of the stone, surrounding the other man in a cage. It was not an ordinary cage; it was exceptionally thick and would take a great amount of force to destroy.

In addition, vines wrapped around his hands tying the fingers together before thick wood surrounded each one. He would not be making any more hand signs anything soon.

He shifted his eyes over to Yoshiaki, "About time you stopped fooling around."

"Your wife was rather insistent on watching you," he gave a shrug. "How could I refuse?"

Kioshi sank down to one knee, breathing hard. He had lost a lot of chakra in the fight. He narrowed his gaze on the man that was trapped in Yoshiaki's cage. He wanted nothing more than to kill him but now, he was not sure how he could do so. His regenerative powers were far too great.

"What shall we do with him?"

"For now, we will have to take him back with us. We will let Naozumi make that decision."

Yoshiaki raised a brow at him, "Really?"

Kioshi came back to his feet, "If I knew how to kill him, I would, believe it. Naozumi will know how to deal with him in a way that will be lasting."

"Let me out and fight me, you coward!" Draidan yelled, slamming his bound hands against the wooden beams of his prison.

"Settle down, we will deal with you soon enough," Kioshi answered in his bored tone.

This seemed to enrage him even more. Kioshi grinned beneath his mask as the other man tried hitting the sides, top, and bottom looking for any kind of weakness in his fury. He was thankful Yoshiaki was with him. He would have found his weakness eventually. Everyone had a weakness; it was just a matter of finding it.

He did not like having to turn the matter over to Naozumi. The anger rolling beneath his surface as he looked at the man was primal. It was beyond fury. He had a feeling that once he got an even better look at Raven he was going to be beyond livid, and there was not much he could do about it. Not without figuring out how to get around his regenerative power.

Kioshi clinched his hand into a fist. The only outward indication he allowed to be shown of the fury still brimming beneath the surface.

Raven felt her eyes getting very heavy as they sailed through the trees. The speed was beyond human, obviously powered by chakra. She felt her head roll to the side onto his shoulder. It had become so heavy.

"Stay awake," the young man carrying her said as he raced through the forest.

She blinked, straining to do as she was commanded. She managed to get her eyes open, but she could not raise her head. "I'm awake," she finally spoke.

All she could do is stare at his mask, ear, and neck. His hair was a dark blond and a little curly at the nape. The mask he wore was that of an owl and decorated in greens and gold. She shifted her gaze down and frowned slightly. His body was muscular but in a lanky sort of way. She had the distinct impression that he was very young for a Shadow guard. She would even venture a guess that he was still a teenager.

She suddenly felt very old.

"I'm so tired."

"Stay awake," he repeated.

She almost laughed at the tone. It reminded her of Kioshi the way he said it. She grinned, feeling better for the future knowing that there would be others coming up behind them that would continue the path they made.

"Thank you," she said while fighting to keep her eyes open. "I appreciate your assistance."

The mask turned towards her. She noticed that his eyes were such a shade of blue that they looked silver. He turned away from her to focus forward. It had obviously surprised him that she had thanked him.

"We will be at the village shortly," he responded in that same monotone he had been using.

"That's good," she mumbled. "I don't know how much longer I can keep my eyes open. Too much blood."

He looked down at her then seemed to speed up even more. Everything was becoming a green streak as they sailed through the trees back to the village. He was very fast. She almost wondered if he was faster than Kioshi.

Somehow, she managed to keep her eyes open the whole trip. Her limbs were feeling numb by the time they got to the hospital. The Shadow guard passed her off and disappeared from her sight as they took her to the back.

She felt warmth enter her body as the medics placed their hands over her wounds. She groaned as she felt the inner wounds slowly healing and closing. It was the strangest sensation and still a bit painful even with the non-invasive technique.

"She needs blood," the medic that was healing the sword wound to her abdomen stated. "She's too low."

"On it," another medic said.

Raven flinched as an IV was stuck in her arm for a blood transfusion. She could feel herself getting stronger as the blood transferred into her. The chill that had fallen over her was receding as well. Another strange sensation fell upon her as well. She felt as if she could sense something on another level of awareness.

"You're going to be fine," the medic that had their hands over her abdomen said while looking down at her. "Everything is closing up good."

Ten minutes later, she was sitting up in bed. The worst of her injuries repaired. Her face was still swollen but since it was not life threatening, they had just given her a cold compress to hold over it. Her hands were cut up pretty good as well. The deeper cuts they had healed but the smaller ones, they left to heal on their own.

She looked at them and grimaced. Most of the damage had been self-inflicted as she had fought against being taken by the man who had found her hiding place. It was strange but she felt a measure of pride at how hard she had fought. She did not think she had it in herself.

She had been taken to central command once she had been released from the medic corps care. The strangest sensations were falling over her. She felt like something inside herself had been opened. She shook her head, holding the cold compress to the side of her face. Was she losing it?

Raven felt a wave of energy roll over her. Something powerful was coming her way. How did she know that? A moment later, Naozumi came into the room she was waiting in. His blue eyes had concern, but she could also almost see the power he held brimming beneath the surface.

He looked like he was going to say something, but then he paused and tilted his head to the side. "Something is different with you." He placed his hand on her shoulder, "Amazing. Your chakra is surging, Raven. I don't know what happened, but I can feel it inside of you."

She looked at him with wide eyes, "That must be why I could feel you coming."

"Interesting... We will have to look into what might have caused this to happen." He shook his head, remembering why he had come before getting distracted. "I wanted to let you know, our teams reached Kioshi and Yoshiaki. They're on their way here now and they have your abductor captured."

Raven gave a heavy sigh of relief, "Thank God."

"Also..."

The door opened and Hikari came in with her babies. She started crying as she took one then the other from her. She could not stop kissing them.

"Thank you, thank you, thank you," she whispered repeatedly. "I knew they were safe with you."

"Oh my, Raven, your chakra!" Hikari exclaimed after starting at her for a moment. "It looks like ours!"

Naozumi glared at the man that had been brought in caged in one of Yoshiaki's traps. He had not only physically harmed Raven and Kioshi, he had destroyed parts of the village and injured some of the citizens. His blue eyes glowed with the anger he was feeling. Kioshi and Yoshiaki stood silently to the side as he weighted his decision. Shinjiro stood to the right of him silently.

"What is your recommendation, Shinjiro?"

"We could find a way to execute him, but it would be a real pain," he finally stated. "We could confine him at Ridgeback. Granted he is not one of our own, but it is the most secure place that we have. With the right kind of restraints, we should be able to keep him locked away for the rest of his life."

Naozumi narrowed his eyes, clearly mulling over which direction he would go. He folded his arms in front of his chest and shifted his gaze to Kioshi.

"You are certain you want to leave this decision to me?"

"I would prefer to kill him straight away but seeing as how that is not an option right now, I defer to your judgement."

Naozumi gave a nod of his head. "We will keep him at Ridgeback; however, I want a team to work on means by which we can deal with those that possess this sort of power. If they can find a solution, I will re-evaluate his position at that time."

Kioshi gave him a thankful nod.
Naozumi looked at Shinjiro, "Make sure that he
is heavily guarded, just in case his men think to
try to release him on the journey there."

"What a pain," Shinjiro muttered.

Kioshi hesitated outside the door to
where Raven had been left to wait. His emotions
were almost overwhelming. Twice now he had
almost lost her, but miraculously she had come
through both experiences. By his history, he
should have lost her. He closed his eyes, feeling
for the first time as if perhaps he was not a
harbinger of death after all. Somehow, some
way, she had broken the curse that had hung over
him like a noose.

The door swung open suddenly and she
was standing there looking up at him. His heart
ached as he looked at the side of her face that
was swollen, but her eyes were smiling at him.

"How long were you planning on
standing outside this door instead of coming in
and kissing me?"

Kioshi laughed and scooped her up.
"You're going to be the death of me, Raven."

He framed her face with his hands then
kissed her like a man that was dying. After a few
moments, she laughed as little hands were tugging
on both of their pants. He pulled back and
looked down.

Oshin was standing steady with his hands
raised up. Kioshi laughed and picked him up
eagerly. The boy squealed at the fast lift into the
air. Raven reached down and picked up Kai. As

she looked at her husband, she felt such complete peace.

"I'm taking a vacation," Kioshi announced as they left the building. "It seems that every time I leave, something happens. I need a break. My old bones just can't take all of this excitement."

They were silent as they walked home. Kioshi could feel the effects of the battle. It was not the most intense battle he had ever fought but it had made an impact. He just was not as young as he used to be. He looked down at Raven as they reached their home. It would not matter how old he got, he would always do everything he could or take any kind of physical damage if it meant protecting her. He could not believe the depths of his feelings towards her or how he almost had pushed her out of his life from fear.

Kioshi looked down at his son, who had fallen asleep on the walk home. His little head was on his shoulder, it made his heart soften. He then looked at Kai, who Raven was laying down in the crib. She was going to be a heartache when she got older, he just felt it. Yet he would not trade her for anything either.

Carefully he laid Oshin down into the crib, to not wake him. Raven slid her hand in his own and tugged him back out of the room to the living room.

"Let me look you over," she said softly. "I know you didn't bother getting the medics to check you out."

"I'm fine, just a little beat up."

"Sit," she ordered.

He raised his hands in surrender before sinking into the chair she had pointed to. He could not stop the wince as his side gave a sharp stab of pain from what he assumed was bruised ribs. She gave him an unreadable look before extending her hands to him. As he gave her his hands, she took one glove off and carefully looked his hand over. She kissed his knuckles, which were bruised from the fight. She then took the other glove off, repeating the process.

Raven then reached up and unbound his headband. She gently ran her fingers through his hair, as if inspecting his head for any injuries yet it was beginning to stir his loins. He had half a mind to drag her across his lap. She then pulled his face mask off and stared at him for a long time.

"I'll never get over how handsome you are," she said after a long moment.

She then leaned close as she inspected his face and neck for any injuries. He reached for her and she laughed, stepping back and shaking a finger at him.

"Oh no you don't," she laughed. "I'm going to inspect you before any loving."

Kioshi groaned and rolled his eyes, "Raven, you're killing me here."

A devilish gleam entered her eyes, "All in good time. Just be patient, you can have your way after I'm done."

Raven almost laughed again at the expression he was giving her right then. She stepped towards him when he settled back once more. "Can you take off your shirt, please?"

She had to bite her lip when he pulled it off a little too eagerly before tossing it to the side. She felt a twinge of emotions as she looked at his torso. He was a patchwork of scars, visible reminders to the dangerous life he had lived. She winced as she saw his entire right side was discolored. She knelt down in front of him to look closer at it. Gently she touched the injury, he hissed in his breath.

Her eyes burned, wanting to cry. In that moment, she fully realized how much physical pain had been inflicted on him in his life. His torso was a patchwork of scars. While the injury to his side would leave no scar, it was a testament to how much the man she loved had endured. This time, on her behalf.

Kioshi was wordless as he watched her lean forward to gently kiss his bruised side. "I'm so sorry," she whispered, a tear rolling over her cheek. He would have said something more but she had moved her lips to an older scar, kissing it next. He was mesmerized as she repeated the action for every scar on his torso. His arousal at the action was noticeable. He somehow managed to restrain himself from taking the control back.

He closed his eyes, unable to watch her without losing his cool. Her lips were soft against his flesh and he gave an involuntary groan as her tongue darted out to trace some of the scars. The pain to his side was forgotten. He almost came up out of the seat as her lips gently sucked the skin just above the hem of his pants.

"Raven..." he groaned as he opened his eyes.

Her eyes were green in color as she looked up at him with a knowing smile. "I want to make you forget about every pain you've ever known."

Kioshi sucked in his breath as she unbuttoned his pants, releasing his aching manhood. "Oh god," he breathed out as her mouth enveloped him. He threaded his fingers through her hair as pleasure overwhelmed him. Her mouth was working him so good, he thought for a moment it would almost kill him in sweet agony.

He pulled her head back when he almost lost it. He quickly pulled her up to her feet to discard her pants, then brought her back down to straddle him. He groaned as she met his thrust upward, her warmth enveloping him tightly. He flexed his fingers on her hips as she rode him.

"Open your shirt," he groaned. "I want to see you."

Raven quickly unbuttoned her shirt as he continued to guide her up and down his shaft. The moment her breasts were free, he captured one then the other between his lips. Kioshi groaned, secured her legs about his waist before taking them both to the ground. He needed to be closer.

She felt like heaven beneath him as he ground into her. He could feel her reaching her climax before she ever called out his name. He thrust harder into her before pouring himself into her, the release purifying.

Kioshi breathed heavily, her scent intoxicating. He raised his head to look down at her.

Raven was stunned as she noticed moisture on either cheek from tears. He smiled at her, "Don't you know? You have already made me forget all those years of solitude and pain. You ended my curse of being a harbinger of death. I love you so much, Raven."

She felt her own eyes burn at the words. "I love you so much too, Kioshi. You healed my broken heart before I even met you. I'm so thankful that I was brought here. You are my greatest love."

Kioshi gave her one of those mind blowing kisses. "Since the kids are still asleep... we should have another go."

His stamina never ceased to surprise her.

Sarah Hatake

Epilogue

Four Years Later...

Raven could not be prouder than she was as she watched her son, Oshin, and daughter, Kia, being inducted into the academy. Kioshi's arm was draped across her shoulders. From the corner of her eye, she could see that his eyes were crinkled in that delightful way that she loved as he watched his children.

Oshin was the spitting image of his father at that age. The only difference was his eyes were blue, the same as her father's. Raven shifted the baby on her hip.

Zane Hamasaki had been the biggest surprise for them. He was not supposed to be born as they had disconnected her tubes after nearly dying with the twins. She had a cyst bust on her ovary, an egg slipped out, and the rest was history. Her pregnancy with him was vastly different than the pregnancy with the twins.

To everyone's shock, the blood transfusion she had received after being kidnapped had an unusual side effect. Her chakra was altered to match that of those in this dimension. She had been reminded of the saying that "life is in the blood." Zane was a perfectly normal pregnancy.

Kioshi had been a nervous wreck until it was clear that her pregnancy with Zane would not be a repeat of the twins. Once that happened, he had relaxed and it had been sweet to watch him as he talked to the baby inside of her. Sometimes he would sing to him. He did all the things he was unable to do with the twins since he had been away on mission.

Raven could barely remember life before coming to the village. She still had her pictures, which she would look at from time to time. The music that she enjoyed, she still listened to it. Yet the pain, the loneliness of her former life was gone. She had found her true home.